What was he going to do? Was he going to kill her—strangle her, perhaps? Why wasn't she frightened? Why didn't she run or scream? Why did she have to stand rooted to this spot on the old kitchen linoleum, with the chops burning on the gas range and no power in her hands or feet to go and save them? And those awful words! Would she ever forget them if she lived beyond this terrible moment? They shivered through her like keen blades. He was coming nearer still. He had taken two more steps. She could smell the liquor on his breath. Would it ever end, this awful waiting for him to do his worst?

Tyndale House books by Grace Livingston Hill.
Check with your area bookstore for these best-sellers.

LIVING BOOKS®

1 *Where Two Ways Met*
2 *Bright Arrows*
3 *A Girl To Come Home To*
4 *Amorelle*
5 *Kerry*
6 *All Through the Night*
7 *The Best Man*
8 *Ariel Custer*
9 *The Girl of the Woods*
10 *Crimson Roses*
11 *More Than Conqueror*
12 *Head of the House*
14 *Stranger within the Gates*
15 *Marigold*
16 *Rainbow Cottage*
17 *Maris*
18 *Brentwood*
19 *Daphne Deane*
20 *The Substitute Guest*
21 *The War Romance of the Salvation Army*
22 *Rose Galbraith*
23 *Time of the Singing of Birds*
24 *By Way of the Silverthorns*
25 *Sunrise*
26 *The Seventh Hour*
27 *April Gold*
28 *White Orchids*
29 *Homing*
30 *Matched Pearls*
32 *Coming Through the Rye*
33 *Happiness Hill*
34 *The Patch of Blue*
36 *Patricia*
37 *Silver Wings*
38 *Spice Box*
39 *The Search*
40 *The Tryst*
41 *Blue Ruin*
42 *A New Name*
43 *Dawn of the Morning*
44 *The Beloved Stranger*
45 *The Gold Shoe*
46 *Through These Fires*
47 *The Street of the City*
48 *Beauty for Ashes*
49 *The Enchanted Barn*
50 *The Finding of Jasper Holt*
51 *The Red Signal*
52 *Tomorrow About This Time*
53 *Job's Niece*
54 *The Obsession of Victoria Gracen*
55 *Ladybird*
56 *The Prodigal Girl*
57 *The Honor Girl*
58 *The Chance of a Lifetime*
59 *Astra*
60 *Miranda*
61 *Mystery Flowers*
63 *The Man of the Desert*
64 *Miss Lavinia's Call*
65 *An Unwilling Guest*
66 *The Girl from Montana*
67 *A Daily Rate*
68 *The Story of a Whim*
69 *According to the Pattern*
70 *In the Way*
71 *Exit Betty*
72 *The White Lady*
73 *Not Under the Law*
77 *The Ransom*
78 *Found Treasure*
79 *The Big Blue Soldier*
80 *The Challengers*
81 *Duskin*
82 *The White Flower*
83 *Marcia Schuyler*
84 *Cloudy Jewel*
85 *Crimson Mountain*
86 *The Mystery of Mary*
87 *Out of the Storm*
88 *Phoebe Deane*
89 *Re-Creations*
90 *Sound of the Trumpet*
91 *A Voice in the Wilderness*
92 *The Honeymoon House*
93 *Katharine's Yesterday*

THE HONOR GIRL

LIVING BOOKS®
Tyndale House Publishers, Inc.
Wheaton, Illinois

This Tyndale House book
by Grace Livingston Hill
contains the complete text
of the original hardcover edition.
NOT ONE WORD
HAS BEEN OMITTED.

Printing History
J. B. Lippincott edition published 1927
Bantam edition/1980
Tyndale edition/1993

Cover artwork © 1993 by Bruce Emmett

Library of Congress Catalog Card Number 93-93862
ISBN 0-8423-1390-7

Printed in the United States of America

99 98 97 96 95 94
8 7 6 5 4 3 2

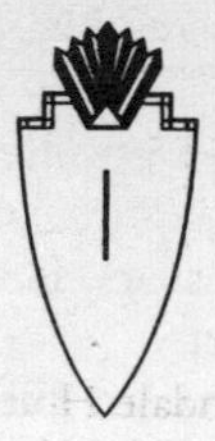

THERE was an audible hush, even above the tinkling notes of the piano, as Elsie stepped out upon the floor of the gymnasium and bowed to her audience.

This was the *pièce de résistance* of the programme, and every eye was fastened upon the girl who had carried off honors in more directions than any other girl in school. She had gone beyond mere speculation or jealousy, and had become the admiration of the girls, the pride of the teachers. They delighted in her every achievement. Whatever she did, whether to lead in a debate, to work out a difficult problem in mathematics, or to translate some obstruse sentence in Latin, they settled into silence and prepared to be entertained. That she had recently discovered a new gift of nature in the line of athletics was the crowning pleasure of her friends. And now upon the occasion of the annual Maypole Dance, given by the members of the gymnasium classes, Elsie Hathaway was to be distinguished anew. The audience settled into instant quiet, with pleased expectation upon every face.

There were present many distinguished men and women, parents and friends of the school, the smiling members of the Faculty, a goodly company of students from the near-by men's college, and even a sprinkling of gray-haired college professors. It was an audience worthy of anyone's best efforts.

Just above the platform in the gallery sat Professor Bowen, the principal of the school, gray-haired, dignified, scholarly, with gentleness and kindliness written all over his strong, true face.

By his side sat a stranger, a former pupil in another school, a most attractive youth so far as looks were concerned, who had stopped over for a day to visit his old friend and teacher who had been his greatest inspiration during high school days.

Most of the programme was over. The tall, white-robed queen with flowing hair, and wreaths of simlax and asparagus fern, like emerald frost-work over her white garments, had marched in with her fairy attendants dressed in all manner of fantastic costumes. They had placed her upon the throne, crowned her, danced about her and the Maypole; danced separately and together; danced with pink and blue and white ribbons around and around the pole until it stood sheathed in its woven rainbow.

Cameron Stewart, at first amused by the brilliant, ever-changing panorama, had begun furtively to count the remaining numbers on the programme and wish that he and his dear Professor Bowen might slip away and have a good old-time talk. There were hosts of questions he wanted to ask, and as many things he wanted to tell, and here they had to sit and watch these girls playing like giddy butterflies. After all there was a good deal about girls' schools that was like child's play, he thought. Nonsense. You wouldn't catch men wasting their time on fol-de-rols like that. He wondered that Professor Bowen could care to sit through it all. He was not even one of the judges, why did he not slip out? Would it do to suggest it? He must take that early train in the morning, if possible, and there would be so little time to talk after this performance was over!

He cast a furtive glance at Professor Bowen to see if a suggestion of this kind would be welcome, but he saw on the old, kindly face an expression of deep interest, expectation, and satisfaction—the same that used to bloom for himself sometimes when he had done well at school, the look he had met when he stood up to deliver the valedictory. It had stirred his heart to its depths and had been his inspiration during that long and carefully prepared speech, helping him to put the right fire into his words. The interest in that kindly face had been one of the long-cherished pictures on the walls of his memory. And was it possible that it could be worn for the sake of a foolish dancing girl? It was worth nothing then. It was but put on to please! He must tear the picture down from that most honored place in his heart and memory and realize that he was growing up and that nothing was as it had seemed when he was a boy. He was conscious of a distinct twinge of disappointment and jealousy, as with a deep, involuntary sigh he turned to see what or who had the power to bring out the look which of old had not sat upon that noble face for nothing.

Elsie Hathaway stood poised for an instant, surveying her audience, cool, self-possessed, lovely, a veritable fairy in her make-up.

She was small and slight, a dainty head set upon dainty shoulders, her garments green, soft and fluffy. Even her slippers were apple green and her gown of green gauze, modest and simple, with a round neck, not too low, and little short puffed sleeves fitted closely to her round, pink arms. The greenness set off the red gold hair. She had taken off the wreath of green roses she had worn when she marched with the queen around the Maypole, and looked as simple as any wood nymph about to dance upon the moss of the forest. She swept a glance over her audience, then looked up in the gallery straight to where the stranger sat with the gray-haired professor, and gave him one cool, questioning glance. Somehow her eyes challenged his interest even against his will. They had so much of quiet assurance for a mere little high school dancer. But he sat up and gave cold, critical attention to the movements of the wood nymph.

She swept her audience a grave, dignified bow, almost too dignified for a wood nymph, he thought. It gave the impression of an intellectual wood nymph, solemnly but sweetly performing some woodland ceremony.

The she moved with the music, light as a thistle-down blown by the wind, fanciful as the sunlight playing with the leaves of the trees and sifting through the branches to the shadowy moss in yellow, twinkling kisses. Her every movement was utmost grace, not the slightest affectation, but perfect self-control, perfect confidence in her own supple power. He watched her as the others did; as anyone would watch a beautiful piece of mechanism; and as he grew less astonished at the beauty of the gliding movements, a perfect poetry of motion, he began to ruminate bitterly on that look on his old professor's face. After all, he reflected, there was the child in every heart, for even an old man would be carried away with a pretty girl dancing. Nevertheless, he watched the whirling bit of feathery green as breathlessly as the rest of the audience, till she at last swept another low bow and glided out of sight and then he turned to see that old face beside him beaming with the same light it had worn when Professor Bowen came to congratulate him upon the honors he had won in high school.

It fell blankly upon the younger man. It brought

bitterness to his soul. He was amazed. He could not bear to find his idol but human after all. A mere dancing puppet, pretty, of course, but after all a puppet! And Professor Bowen! devotee of art and science and literature! But before he could find words to express his disappointment Professor Bowen spoke.

"She's a wonderful little girl!" said he, "brightest student we have had for years! She simply swept the honors away from everyone else."

"In athletics, I suppose!" said the young man, his lip curling sarcastically.

Professor Bowen turned in surprise at the tone and looked his young friend in the face anxiously. That did not sound like his dear Cameron. Was the boy getting the "swelled head" with all his honors?

"Not at all," said Professor Bowen, adjusting his have-to-be-convinced tone of voice that he used in cases of obstreperous or lazy scholars. "She's a wonder in any direction you take her. She's a marvel of keenness in mathematics, quick as a flash in Latin, up in literature and the sciences. I never saw anything like it. She studies early and late, takes little or no time for recreation, and is as sweet and kindly with it all as you ever saw a girl. She was working so hard her health was breaking under it, and we insisted upon her giving some time to the development of her body. She struggled hard against it at first, but I had her up in my study, and had a long talk with her about it, how she would be no good at all if her body broke down, and finally convinced her; this is the result. She plunged into athletics with as much vim as anything else, and put her perfect self-control into tangible form for our pleasure."

"Of course this dancing business is merely to please the gymnasium teacher, but it shows what wonderful power the girl has. She's the best all-around developed student I ever saw, with no exception," the old man finished emphatically.

The younger man bit his lips. He was mortified that he had a rival in his dear old professor's heart. A girl, too, a dancing girl!

"And what good will it all be to her," said the young man, bitterly. "She may dance well and do difficult mathematical problems, and all that, but what will she accomplish? I don't suppose she expects to earn her living by dancing or mathematics, either. She doesn't look it. How will she be any better than other girls? I don't know whether I believe much in higher education for women. It rather unfits them for their after life."

He spoke with the intolerance of youth.

The old professor looked at the young man with keen pity in his eyes. To think that Cameron had got no further than that! He could not see the bitterness in the heart of his young idolator.

"No, she probably will never earn her living by her knowledge, for she will not need to do so. She has a wealthy uncle and is not studying with any such purpose in view. But it is not possible, my dear friend, that you do not think a woman better for every advantage she can have!"

"Oh, no, of course not," said the younger man, half vexed with himself. "But I was wondering that you could be so pleased over a mere pretty frivolity like this. It did not seem like you!"

The old professor smiled.

"I was pleased over the many tests the child has stood and shines in them all. She's a rare girl. She's pure gold. You don't know her."

"Are you sure you do?" asked Stewart, a bit impudently. "After all, these tests are not real. It's the after life that is the real test, the home life."

"Some who have taken such honors in school have been tried by fire and they have shone out pure gold, Cameron," said the old professor, his voice trembling slightly. He could call to mind instances that brought tears to his old eyes.

"Well, I'd like to see this paragon of yours tried by fire once—the fire in the range, for instance. If she could stand that she surely ought to be the honor girl," laughed the young man. And looking down, as if drawn by some strange attraction, he met the eyes of Elsie Hathaway, clear, keen, haughty, and he knew that she had heard him, for she stood just beneath the low gymnasium gallery.

He felt the color stealing up into his face annoyingly. What was the matter with him? He tried to comfort himself by thinking that she could not possibly know of whom he was speaking but in his heart he was sure she did all the time. Well, she was only a kid anyway, why should he care? He was glad that Professor Bowen started downstairs.

He hoped to escape this marvellous Hathaway kid further, but the professor was determined his two best-beloved pupils should meet and brought about an introduction. Stewart tried to say something about how much he had enjoyed her dancing, but she held him coolly with her eyes, and turning away talked to Professor Bowen. Cameron Stewart was glad when he at length emerged from the crowd of eager, fluttering schoolgirls, and gray, smiling elderly teachers, and was seated in the big leather chair of his beloved professor's study. But somehow after he was there he could not think of the things he had intended to say and he found himself listening to a long tale of Elsie Hathaway's achievements, told by the dear old man who could not bear to have his pet pupil discounted.

Elsie Hathaway, cool, dainty, lovely, dividing the honors with the queen of the occasion, moved down the length of the gymnasium slowly, met on every hand by adulation.

"O Elsie, you dear, you were too sweet!" murmured another girl snuggling up to her, proud to be allowed to stay a few minutes by her side.

"Elsie Hathaway, we are proud to lay even the honors of the Athletic Department at your feet," saluted a teacher bending to fasten a decoration of fluttering ribbons and gleaming stones on Elsie's green gauze breast.

They gathered around her, laughing and chattering as only schoolgirls can chatter. Now and then the group would be broken into by friends who wished to be introduced and tell how much they had enjoyed the beautiful entertainment Elsie had given them; and little girls who had been privileged witnesses looked wonderingly at the fairy who was real flesh and blood, after all.

They gave her flowers, they invited her to dine, they showered their compliments freely, as Elsie progressed to the door of the gymnasium, and outside it was the same.

The boys from the neighboring college stood hovering in shadowy groups along the way, watching for her coming with admiring glances.

"Say, that was something great, Elsie! You'd make your fortune on the stage. What a pity so much talent is lost to the public!" said a daring youth.

"It certainly was fine, Elsie. I never saw anything more graceful in my life. Butterflies aren't in it with you, nor a bird on the wing. I didn't know, one whirl there, but you had been growing some wings yourself and might fly away from us!" chimed in another, gallantly.

"Say, Elsie, that was dandy!" called out a young man who presumed upon a distant cousinship.

And so, laughing and admiring they accompanied her to her uncle's car where awaited her proud aunt and uncle and two adoring cousins, and as they drove away a low admiring murmur of friendly voices, almost like a cheer, followed her into the night.

One might have expected Elsie's head to be turned, and she certainly was pleased with all the pleasant things that had been said to her. One drop of bitter was mixed with the sweet, however, perhaps to make the sweet seem all the sweeter.

The beloved aunt and two dear cousins fluttered after her even to her room and stayed to talk over the evening, how everyone did, and what everyone said. They told her as they left that she had been the best of all. But it all surged over her after they were gone, that one bitter drop in the evening's draught of delight.

"Horrid thing I hate him!" she said to herself in the glass. "He just spoiled it all for me. He had an awfully supercilious look. He said he would like to see me 'tried by the fire in the range.' I know he was talking about me. His eyes were too honest to keep me from knowing, though his tongue did try to make me think he had enjoyed it, and deceive me about what he had said. He is one of those old-fashioned men who want to keep women down to their 'sphere,' I'm sure. Poor fellow! He belongs to a former generation. Well, I'm thankful I don't have to make fires in ranges nor be tried by them, but if I did, and had to, I'm sure I could excel if I tried. Anyway, I'd like to show that man that I could—and I know I could. I wish they had courses in ranges at school and I'd take one just to prove to the horrid fellow that I could do something in that line, too. It's my opinion people can do well in anything if they only put their hearts into it, no matter what it is. It may not be so pleasant, but they can make it a means of winning. Dear old Professor Bowen! He thought I was pure gold. I wonder if I am?"

And so she fell asleep.

But the fire that was to try Elsie Hathaway was not far away.

WHEN Elsie awoke the next morning, which was Saturday, everything looked bright in her life. She had forgotten the hateful stranger. He was relegated to the place in her mind with farmers who worked their wives to death, and prosaic men who saw no good in women except to do drudgery. She remembered only the delightful things that had been said, and the intoxication of the whirling, gliding motion of her dance the night before. If it were right and not frivolous and useless she would delight to go on entertaining people in that way always. It was a delicious sensation to feel herself floating to the music, in the sight of admiring beholders, and to know that she had the power to charm them thus. She felt that the intoxication was dangerous and it was well the gymnasium was closed with last night's performance. There would be no more temptation that year for showing off. She must look out for herself not to let that tendency grow. Of all things she despised people who thought too much of themselves. But there would probably be no danger in that sort of thing next year. She would be a senior and would have to work. This had but been a play and now it was over.

With which sensible reflections she put the finishing pat to a charming costume and went down to breakfast in a cool muslin of palest sea green, the color that always intensified the red gold of her hair and make it shine like a halo. One of the boys used to say that Elsie Hathaway was the only girl in the world who looked better with light golden eyelashes than she would have done with dark. They seemed but to soften the delicate texture of her skin as white chiffon might do, and made a shy drapery for the grayness of her eyes—eyes that never seemed to flirt or grow boldly intimate. The boys liked her quiet reserve.

And indeed, Elsie Hathaway was well content with life as she had found it the last seven years. She had everything that money could buy or heart could wish, at least within reason, and a home and family whose greatest desire seemed to be to please her, and yet withal they loved her so wholesomely that it had not seemed to spoil her.

When Elsie's mother had died Elsie was a slim little girl of eight and her aunt and uncle had taken her at once to the city to live with them. There had been a faithful old colored servant at her father's home to keep the house running for Mr. Hathaway and Elsie's two brothers, and there had been no question at all but that Elsie should go to live with her aunt. Her father had accepted passively his sister-in-law's decision that a girl at Elsie's age needed a mother's care. Mr. Hathaway was crushed by the death of his wife and seemed not to be able to plan anything for himself.

Aunt Esther's home had been wonderful, and Elsie had been made welcome to share all its comforts and luxuries with her two cousins, Katharine and Bettina, and so the happy school years had passed, finding her at the close of her junior year in high school, and full of honors and happiness. She still made her home with her aunt and uncle for they would hear of nothing else. Indeed, she had so grown into the life of the home in the city that it never occurred to her that she might not always be there, or that there was anything else for her to do. She loved them all and they loved her and wanted her. It was her home, as much as if she had been born there. That was the whole story. She loved them all, she loved the life they led, the friends they had, the concerts and lectures they attended, the beautiful summers at the seashore and mountains, she loved the church in which they had their affiliations, and she rejoiced that her lot had fallen in such pleasant places.

During those years she had seen very little of her first home, and had gradually grown farther and farther from both father and brothers until they seemed more like distant relatives than her own blood. They seldom came to see her, and her life was so full and so happy that she had little time to go to them or even to think about them.

The last time she had seen her father he had asked her how she would like to come home and keep house for him, and she shuddered inwardly at the very thought, although she told him gayly how impossible it was. That was three months ago. Her father had sighed and looked old. His breath smelled of liquor, and he was continually smoking an ugly little black pipe. She shrank from him as if he had not been her father. Uncle James was not like that. He was pleasant, and he never drank. She tried to forget her father as much as possible. As for her brothers she scarcely felt that they belonged to her, even distantly. And the days had been so full and so happy that it had been easy to forget.

The sun was shining brightly and the breakfast was very gay and festive. Waffles and honey and strawberries, and all the talk ran upon last night—what this one and that one had said about Elsie. Uncle James even had a word to quote from Professor Bowen.

"He called you the Honor Girl, Elsie!" said he, "I must say when he got done praising you I began to feel that I ought to be very much honored that I belonged to you. Why, according to your principal you have taken the cake with all the frosting away from everyone else in town."

There was a merry twinkle in her uncle's eyes, but she knew that behind all his teasing there was a loving pride in her accomplishments, and her heart swelled with joy. She felt that this was a glorious day, the crown of all the days that had passed before.

The girls had planned to play tennis at the country club that morning, so after breakfast was over and her uncle had gone down to his office, they went up to their rooms to dress for their game.

"Elsie," called Katharine from her room, "did you find that book of poems yet? I simply have to have it for to-morrow. I promised Miss Keith I would bring it to Sunday School. She wants to quote it in an article she is writing, and she needs to send it off Monday."

"No, Katharine," said Elsie, "I didn't find it. But I am afraid I must have left it out at Father's house—"she always spoke of her former home as "Father's house" now—"I remember I was learning a poem out of it the last time I went out there, and I'm sure I left it up on my little old bureau."

"Oh, how tiresome!" said Katharine. "Now, what will I do?"

"Oh, that's easy. I'll run out there right after the game."

"But the concert! You'll be late for the concert I'm afraid. Those trolleys are so slow! What a pity Daddy had to use the car this morning. We could have gone out in no time."

"Oh, it won't take me long if I go right in on the bus from the Club House. Don't worry! I'll get it for you, kitten," said Elsie cheerfully. She felt she could do almost anything to-day, she was so very happy.

In her pretty little sports dress of white jersey trimmed with jade and a close white felt hat, she started out with her cousins, Katharine in pink and Bettina in pale blue, their rackets under their arms, and happiness upon their faces. Elsie carried also a book to read on her long ride out to Morningside where her father's house was located.

"We'd go with you," said Katharine, "only Mamma said we had to finish those things for the bazaar this morning or we couldn't go to the concert, you know—" said Bettina wistfully as they parted at the corner where the bus line and trolley crossed.

"Oh, surely!" said Elsie, "I don't mind. I'll soon be home again. Work hard and have your embroidery all done by the time I get there."

And so Elsie was on her way out to her old home to get the book she had left there three months before. In her heart she felt a secret shame for she knew she had chosen this hour for going partly because her father and brothers would not be there.

She did not wish to encounter her father's request again; there had been something hungry in his face, which she had not analyzed at the time, that had made her uncomfortable, disturbed the harmony of her life-setting.

The book she was reading held her interest all the way out to the suburb where was the old home in which she had been born. The climax of her story was reached just as the conductor called out her street and she closed her book with a start and hurried out of the car, not even glancing from the window as she went.

She had little interest in the old place. She was only anxious to complete her errand and hurry away before anybody should return to detain her, for she had planned to go with Bettina and Katharine to the symphony concert that afternoon, and she wanted to get back before lunch.

The house was gray stone and shingle, and stood knee-deep in straggling grass and overgrown vines. It presented a startling neglected look in the bright sunlight as the girl walked up the gravel path. She frowned, and wondered why her brothers did not cut the lawn, train the vines, and clean the edges of the walk. It was disgraceful to let things go this way. She felt a thrill of thankfulness that she did not live in such a run-down home. What a contrast to Aunt Esther's trig, comfortable house in the city!

She paused at the steps, and took note of several things that displeased her. One of the boards in the lower step was rotted away at one end, and the whole gave when her foot touched it. The paint was all off the porch and steps. Three old porch rockers in various stages of dejection stood about in position for the feet of a possible occupant to rest on the weather-beaten railing of the porch. The vines had clambered unchecked over floor and railing alike, adding to the general clutter. Three or four Sunday supplements were scattered about on the floor of the porch and several others matted like a cushion in an old bottomless rocker. Gathering her skirts about her daintily, the daughter of the house made her way disdainfully through the dismal approach and tried the front door. It was locked. She rang the bell several times, with no result. Then she stooped and lifted the old door mat. There was the key in its old place. It seemed to look at her with a pitiful appeal in its worn rusty way. She picked it quickly from the accumulated dust and fitted it into the lock, a great distaste in her soul for the entrance she was about to make into the home of her childhood. She did not like to think that here had been her beginning of life.

She wondered as she threw the door open what had become of Rebecca? Inside the door she paused in dismay. Everything was dirt and disorder. Desolation came to meet her at the threshold.

The pleasant square hall that she remembered as a child mocked at her out of its ruin. The door of the hall closet stood open and hooks and floor bulged with their contents. Overcoats, a roll of carpet, two dilapidated raincoats, three old straw hats, and some felt ones, a stringless tennis racket, an old moth-eaten football suit, and a broken umbrella, all in a heterogeneous mass. The big wooden ball from the top of the newel post lolled in a corner amid rolls of dust. The little couch fairly groaned with more coats and hats. It seemed as if several persons' entire wardrobe must be piled upon this single article of furniture. The window seat was piled with books and papers all mixed up together, with burned matches and ends of cigarettes among them. A picture with a broken glass stood behind the hall table, adding desolation to the scene.

Through the wide doorway the dining table could be seen, covered with a torn, much soiled table cloth, and piled high with soiled dishes bearing traces of fried eggs, bacon, apple cores, and banana skins. A plate in the middle held a single hard end of a baker's loaf. The tin pepper box from the kitchen stood in the middle of the table and a lump of salt lay on the cloth beside it. Neckties and soiled collars appeared on the sideboard, window seats and chairs.

In dismay Elsie turned to the living-room on her right, but confusion also reigned there. More Sunday supplements littered the floor. A bundle of laundry half open lay in a chair. A man's new gray felt hat hung on the broken shade of the lamp on the centre table. The piano—her piano on which she had first picked out her scales, and then with one finger played haltingly "The Star Spangled Banner" was closed and covered with dust. Half a dozen pieces of ragtime, illumined jazzily, stood on the rack, and an old overcoat had been thrown over the top upsetting a Dresden shepherdess vase containing ancient hydrangeas, dry and crumbling.

With an expression of disgust on her face she turned to flee upstairs, get her book and depart as quickly as possible. To think that this was her home! The house where she was born! The place where her father and brothers still lived. To think that her own flesh and blood were satisfied to live like this. It was too dreadful! What if those people last night could have had a glimpse of this, just before her performance? Would they have given her as much praise?

Then with sudden determination to know the worst, Elsie went through the dining-room to the kitchen beyond.

Confusion and destruction met her gaze. A gaunt cat greeted her with a weak protest from a hunched up position on the kitchen table beside the débris of a hasty breakfast wherein eggs had played a prominent part. A bottle half filled with thick milk long past the stage of sourness stood on the dresser menacing the atmosphere with its green and pink coloring. The old sink clogged and half filled with waste water fairly reeked with bits of garbage from the last attempt at dish washing. The cooking utensils on the cold range were filled with sticky messes of varying ages and stages, some burned almost beyond recognition, some sour mashed potatoes, some pasty stewed tomatoes filled with soggy bread, some cannèd corn burned to the sauce pan, its empty can still on the back of the range.

Sick at heart the girl drew back the bolt of the outer kitchen to let in the air. The cat sprang down and hauled from behind the refrigerator a bit of old dried fish with a stench unspeakable, and began to gnaw at it starvedly. Outside the back door a company of dogs were holding high carnival over the forlorn upturned garbage pail.

Elsie slammed the kitchen door shut again and retreated, wondering frantically whether she could catch the next car back. She hurried upstairs shutting her eyes to all the sights.

Her own old room had been at the head of the stairs, opening from the front one belonging to her mother and father. It was the only place in the house where any semblance of order prevailed. Everything was in its place just as she had left it, the bread spread up with an old cover that had once been white. The pictures on the walls, her childish treasures on the bureau, her books in the little bookshelves strung up by cords on the wall, her little rockingchair. Everything was thick with dust, of course; but it seemed to be the only spot in the house where the finger of ruin and despair had not been laid. It was desolate, of course, and utterly unattractive; yet looked like an oasis in the desert compared to the rest of the place.

Elsie found her book, selected one or two others, and turned to go downstairs; but at the top step something compelled her to go back and look into the other rooms. Her father's room, with the bedclothes in a heap, his own garments scattered wildly about, a brandy-flask openly standing on the bureau!

She fled precipitately. Something had caught her eye

hanging over the headboard close by the pillow. Her mother's old dressing-gown of flowered flannelette, faded and torn. Did her father keep it there because it reminded him of her? They had been very fond of each other. Was he lonely? It was the first time the thought had ever occurred to her. She had always pitied herself, a motherless child. She had never thought of him as one to be pitied.

Something forced her to go on and see the rooms.

The bathroom was as desolate as such a spot can become when no one cares for it. Smeared marble black with grime and soap, no towels save two worn soiled ones in a heap on the floor, the oilcloth worn into holes, blacking-brushes and shaving articles strewn inharmoniously together, the window-curtain torn, the door of the medicine-closet hanging by one hinge! Nothing as it ought to be!

She glanced into her elder brother's room. Gene had always been particular. Surely he would have things in some order. But no, the prospect was as dreary as elsewhere, only that there had been an attempt to put the bureau in some kind of order for a row of photographs that held the place of honor there. Elsie stopped to look at them. Girls! Many girls! "Tough girls." Girls with high heels and short skirts, and hair plastered out on their cheeks and forehead after the fashion of the extreme of the day; showing their teeth, languishing with their eyes, and saucily looking into Gene's eyes in some groups. The kind of girls with whom Aunt Esther did not like Katharine, Bettina, and herself to associate. Not bad girls, perhaps, just bold girls, coarse, common girls. With a curl of her lip she went out of the room and shut the door.

What ever made her mount the third-story stairs she did not know. Possibly a desire to see what had become of Rebecca. She pushed open the door of the back room that had formerly belonged to that servant and found no trace of inhabitant. The cot was there on which Rebecca had once slept, an old washstand, and a crooked looking-glass; but the hooks on which Rebecca's garments had hung were vacant. Rebecca had evidently departed. No wonder. Who would want to stay in such a house? Or had the house gone into this state after the departure of Rebecca? Of course, that was it. Rebecca used to keep things in some sort of order, at least.

The front room had been Jack's. He always hated it because he could not stand upright in the corners on account of the sloping roof. He used to protest against the high headboard of his bed that would not allow it to be shoved against the wall. As she passed the little middle storeroom, she caught sight of that headboard and footboard standing back against the wall across the window of the storeroom. Had Jack, then, bought a new bed? She pushed open his door curiously, and her heart sank at the appalling sight.

On the floor in the middle of the room lay the spring and mattress of the great old bed. A single sheet that was torn down the middle, and seemed to have served for months without changing, was the only semblance of bed linen. From the scanty snarl of bedclothes she recognized her mother's old plaid shawl, the only article resembling a blanket. An old overcoat and sweater were in the heap, as if they too had been used for covering. The pillow was guiltless of case and much soiled. It dawned upon her that the stock of bedding and table-linen had likely never been replenished since her mother's death.

Jack's garments hung or lay about the room in wild confusion, one incongruous mass upon floor and chairs and rickety chiffonier. One could hardly step without putting a foot on something. Soiled laundry and clean lay side by side.

The chiffonier was strung across the back with brilliant neckties, and here and there a clean collar brothered with a soiled one. Cigarette stumps and burned matches were literally everywhere. Elsie had never imagined a human being trying to live and sleep in such confusion. She stood stricken in the desolate place, and thought of Jack, with his brave bright eyes and his beautiful crest of wavy golden hair, existing in a room like this. A sudden lump rose in her throat; and she slipped out of the room, and closed the door after her, filled with a kind of shame for her young brother.

She hurried out of the house, closed the door, and locked it, putting the key scrupulously where she had found it, and went out to wait for the car.

She tried to forget the impression she had just received in the house. She tried to think that probably men didn't mind such things; else, why didn't they get some new things, and fix the house up? They were all working and had good salaries. There was no excuse for a state of things like that. Had that been the reason why her father wanted her to come home? Well, she couldn't be a slave to three men in an awful household like that, she who had been so long used to better things, she who had already made a reputation for herself in a small way, young though she was. Was she not the honor girl of Professor Bowen's school?

The car had almost reached the corner where she stood, and she was just about to step down from the curb and signal it, when a sudden remembrance of that room of Jack's in the third story blurred her vision and some invisible hand seemed to draw her back, some voice calling to her, some strange influence touching with vibrant hand her heart-strings. It came to her that she could not leave that room in that condition for Jack to come back to at night. She must go up and try to make things a little more habitable. The others might stand it if they would, but Jack was only a boy. It was dangerous for boys to have no spot in the world that was decent.

She stepped back impulsively, and let the car go by her, then wondered why she had done it. She had no settled purpose, and no distinct idea what she would do. Something seemed compelling her to wait, drawing her back to that pandemonium in the house.

She walked feverishly to the steps again, looking at her watch. If she worked fast, she might be able to catch the next car back to the city; they passed every fifteen minutes. Or the car after that, at least. She could even go without her lunch for once if necessary.

She unlocked the door, and went in again.

The disorder seemed to rush to meet her with more of a shock than at her first entrance, perhaps because her eyes were now open to see it.

She had had it in mind to rush up to Jack's room, shutting her eyes to all else, and put it in quick order that she might catch the next car if possible; but the hall fairly cried out to her for attention. What an entrance home at night for three lonely men! How was it she had never thought of them in this way before?

She stood hesitating a moment, then frantically set to work picking up things.

ELSIE collected the newspapers in a pile, swept the coats from the chairs and couch, hanging them on the empty hooks in the closet, and attacked the window-seat. All those books and papers piled in a heap with a collar and a tie on the top, the old green faded silk curtain pinned back so that the mess was plainly visible from the side street! It took but a minute to straighten the books in a row on the little shelf below the hall table, throw the match-ends, cigar-stumps, and bits of paper into the waste-basket, and remove the collar and a few other alien articles. She seized upon an old napkin over the back of a dining-room chair. It was ragged, but in a state of comparative cleanliness, and would do nicely for a duster. And, when the window-seat was wiped off carefully and the curtain straightened, the sun shone in brightly as if to encourage her with one spot of order at least. Next she turned her attention to the hall table, and began to be interested. It really did not take so long to bring order out of chaos when one went at it in the right spirit.

She went to the kitchen, and dampened her duster

slightly, returning to wipe off the lamp-globe. She shook out the faded silk table-cover, and wondered with a pang whether it might not perhaps have once been one of her mother's treasures. The thought made her handle it more tenderly, and she arranged the table with a few books until that corner at least began to take on a habitable look. The head of the newel drew her attention. She managed to find a hammer, and set it in place, driving the twisted nails back shakily again; and then after a moment's frowning pause she dusted off the old leather couch and attacked the yawning closet. There was no use in trying to make things look nice with that closet door bursting open and sending its contents over the floor.

She looked dubiously down at her pretty dress as she hauled the roll of carpet about. However, it could not be helped now and it would wash. That was a consolation.

Her vigorous efforts soon subdued the closet so that everything was neatly hung up and the door shut. A few old summer hats and coats she put in a pile on the stairs to take up when she went, and, standing back, surveyed her work well pleased. If only the old rug were swept and the edges of the floor wiped around with oil! But she could not stop for everything. They could hire a servant to do that.

She was about to go upstairs when the dining-room asserted itself. Of what use to clean up the hall with a great open doorway into a place like that? The sideboard at least must be tidied.

Doubling her speed, she flew around in the dining-room, straightening and dusting, the pile of things to go upstairs growing larger and larger. She hesitated at the dining-table after removing with uplifted nose and disdainful lips the soiled dishes. Could she leave that dirty tablecloth on? It was stiff with egg and ham gravy, stained with watermelon and peaches and berries, besides being grimy with dust and full of holes. A search in the sideboard revealed two others in like stages of decline. With a sudden set of her lips she bundled them all three together, and put them out in one of the laundry tubs. At least, a bare table was better than dirt.

She dusted everything. The old china-closet with its glass sides and shelves appealed to her strangely. It was almost empty of china and silver and glass. Nearly every dish the house contained seemed to be piled in the kitchen dirty. This china-closet must once have been something of which her mother was proud. A kind of pity for the decadent, inanimate articles of furniture took possession of her as she worked. Somehow she seemed to come nearer to the thought of her mother than she had been since the day of the funeral.

The dining-room at last was set to rights, and she turned to fly upstairs. Two cars had already made their passage cityward since she began, and she must hurry or there would be no time at all for lunch before the concert. But from the dining-room door she had a full view of the unhappy parlor in its grim loneliness, and her heart forbade her to leave it. She must put some semblance of decency into it before she left. Perhaps it would be better to do the parlor and let Jack's room go this time.

She sped to work once more, and soon had straightened the pictures and ornaments on the mantel, removed the hats and coats to places in the hall closet, picked up the papers, placed the chairs invitingly, and dusted. The whole vista was now much more serene than when she had entered the house, but still it was not at all what it ought to be.

"It needs a thorough good housecleaning!" she said

aloud. "And I declare I'd like to do it if I had time! But of course that's out of the question."

She hastened upstairs, passing resolutely by the second story, on up to Jack's room. Somehow the thought of her younger brother had taken strong hold upon her.

She looked about this second time with a kind of determined despair. Where should she start in? How could she accomplish anything? The whole place needed to be shovelled out, and cleansed, and started over again. Why hadn't he taken her room instead of keeping up here where she knew he hated it?

A sudden instinct revealed to her that her room had been left a kind of shrine that kept the desolated home together. Had they hoped she would sometime come back to them, and had left her room as it had been for her? It was a gloomy little room, old-fashioned and small and inconvenient, with nothing valuable in it; but it had been let alone, and her things remained untouched, even when the rest of the family had been in need. The thought pierced into her conscience, and stirred it uneasily from its long contented sleep. Was there, then, a possibility that she ought to have come home, at least sometimes, and been a daughter to the house?

She put the thought ungraciously half defiantly aside, and sailed into that room.

She had to begin at the very entrance, for the floor was literally covered with garments and other articles. She systematically sorted them out. Soiled shirts, cuffs, socks, old shoes and new shoes, overcoats and cast-off neckties galore, of every possible combination of all the colors of the rainbow, old automobile-tires, a book on electrical engineering, several on chemistry, some sporting-papers, a football uniform, a pair of overalls, moth-eaten suits of clothes tumbled down anywhere! It was appalling! And *everywhere* were cigarette-ends and burnt matches. The wonder was the house had not been set on fire. There were several candle-ends on the floor and the chiffonier, and a good many photographs of football and baseball teams scattered about.

Steadily she progressed into the room until she came to the bed and the snarl of queer bedclothes. Then without any warning at all a great lump came to her throat, and the tears rained down her cheeks. To think that her brother should be sleeping in a bed like this, without sufficient clothing to keep him warm and clean, and with no one to care for things and make them comfortable for him after he had been working hard all day!

"For all the world like a drunkard's home!" she said aloud, and choked over the words. Could it be that that was the matter? Could it be that her father really drank much?

She could remember the young brother when she was a little girl, how proud she had been of him. He had had round red cheeks and long golden curls. Her mother had cried when they had to be cut off, and cherished them in a little box put away somewhere now in her own bureau drawer in the little room downstairs. Somehow these remembrances did not serve to stop her tears.

There literally was not any way to make that bed respectable with the material at hand. The old plaid blanket shawl was thin, worn, and torn. The old honeycomb spread that served for an upper sheet was gray with age. The pillow was impossible, and the sheet was in actual shreds. It was fit for nothing but a bonfire. Elsie gathered all in reluctant fingers, trying to think what to do about that bed. She could not put that sheet on again, and she must make up that bed somehow. It would not do for her to take away the only bed Jack had and give him nothing in its place.

At last she had the room in tolerable order, all but the bed. There was a large bundle of soiled things done up for the laundry; the few clean shirts and collars she had found among the débris were arranged neatly in the bureau drawers; the things she did not know what to do with were on the top of the chiffonier, which was dusted; the books were piled in an orderly row against the wall; and the old clothes that needed to be thrown away were collected and put into the empty back room. There was at least clear space to step about in now, and there remained but to make up some kind of a bed. Then she must go.

She looked at her watch. It was five minutes after one. If she could find something down-stairs for the bed, she might get it made up in time to catch the car at twenty-five minutes after one. She could at least get home in time to dress for the concert.

She hurried downstairs, carrying at arm's length a bundle of things which she intended to burn in the back yard; and having set them on fire, she went upstairs again to hunt for sheets and bedclothes.

But the frantic search revealed only more lack in the household fittings. Her father's bed was supplemented by two old coats and a bath-robe. Eugene's had the blankets doubled, and apparently he used only one side of the bed. Several old quilts badly torn and soiled were all she could find in the way of extra bedding, and these were so dilapidated that she put them at once out of the question.

She stood dismayed in the middle of her father's room, and looked about again. How could she go back to her aunt's and sleep in the pretty brass bed that was hers, with its rose blankets, its fine sheets and pillow-cases, its dainty blue silk elder down quilt that had been a recent birthday present from her aunt, and think of her father and brothers lying in squalor and discomfort? She simply could not do it! She could never live with herself again until her conscience had been set at rest about this. She must do something about it.

Investigation in her own former room revealed the fact that there were no sheets or blankets there, only the meagre ancient spread that had once been white, kept there to hold the semblance of a bed for her.

What could have become of all the bedding? Could bedding wear utterly out like that, and disappear? Or could it be that Rebecca or some other servant had carried things off little by little? Well, whatever was the explanation, the things were gone, and others must somehow be provided, or there would be no more peace for her. Moreover, she had discovered that she could no longer be satisfied with clearing up Jack's room, she must also make her father's and Gene's rooms decent before she left. She must, in fact, put the whole of that house into some sort of order, or she could never be happy again; and she must find a way to make those three beds comfortable before night, symphony concert notwithstanding.

Downstairs in her hand-bag was thirty dollars saved from her last birthday present. She had intended using it to have her photograph taken at a famous photographer's. She had meant to indulge in a really artistic photograph, and had saved up for the purpose. But now the money suddenly seemed of more value than the pictures.

At home in a little jewel case locked into her bureau drawer were five twenty dollar gold pieces she had been saving for a long time to purchase an evening cloak. She longed for a really fine one with a handsome fur collar and satin lining. She was going to pick it out the very next week, when her aunt had leisure to go with her and help select it. Suddenly that evening cloak rose and mocked her. Could she wear a gay evening cloak with white fox collar when her own father and brothers had no blankets on their beds?

It is true that they ought to be able to purchase their own blankets, probably were, and would very likely refund any money she would spend on putting the house to rights; at the same time, she must realize that, if she took the responsibility of ordering things without consulting them, she must be ready to pay for them in case they did not approve. There was, moreover, a misgiving about her father's ability to pay for things. What if he had lost his position? What if he had reached a point where he did not care about things? All these things were quite possible when she thought of the state the house had been allowed to get into. Of course she was not responsible; and no one could hold her to blame for the way things had gone; and yet she simply could not go and buy that evening cloak, and know that those beds were in that condition.

She was a girl accustomed to think rapidly and come to quick decisions; and now, as she descended the stairs to the hall, she made her plans.

She washed her hands, locked the door, and went down the street in the direction of the stores. The sight of a colored woman coming toward her gave her another idea. When the woman came near, she stopped her with a question.

"Can you tell me where I can get a couple of women to work for me this afternoon?"

The woman paused, and eyed her reflectively from faultless shoe to dainty hat. Then she shifted to the other hip a bundle of soiled linen which she carried, and replied tentatively:

"Yas'm, I reckon I 'n' my dawter mought. Where to?"

Elsie indicated the house.

There was a surprised rolling of the whites of the old woman's eyes as she swept a quick, comprehensive glance at the house and then back over the girl from top to toe again.

"Dat's Mistah Hathaway's house?" she said with an upward suspicious inflection.

"Yes," said the girl with dignity.

"What you all want done?"

"Oh, cleaning and putting to rights—"

The woman looked her over with a meaningful grunt, growing comprehension in her eyes. Finally she agreed to come and bring her daughter at half past two.

Elsie was hastening on her way when the woman called after her.

"Say, you been't Elsie Hathaway be you? 'Cause I wo'ked fer yer mothah once. She was a mighty nice lady, Mis' Hathaway."

Something warm and disturbing sprang up in the girl's heart and made her smile an assent at the old woman as she hurried on her way again. She seemed to have dropped back years and to be made suddenly aware of the personality of her own dear mother. For a little her life in the city at her aunt's and at the school fell away from her, and she became a child again, interested in this spot that her mother had left. The symphony concert was entirely forgotten now. She had but one object to attain, and that was to put that dreary house into some sort of homelike state before its inhabitants should return. To that end she sought the telephone pay-station, and called up a friend of her aunt's in a large department store.

"Mr. Belknap," she said, "I don't want to make you any trouble, but I'm having a rather strenuous day, and I can't carry out my plans without some help. I'm out at my father's in Morningside, putting the house in order;

and I find that a number of things need replenishing since my last visit. Father isn't here, and I haven't much money with me. I'm wondering if you can manage it for me that they can be sent out special and let me pay on Monday? I could send the money to you as soon as I get home this evening."

"Sure!" came the hearty response. "I can fix that up for you, Miss Elsie. You want the things out this afternoon before you leave? I see. Well, I'll have them run out for you. Just tell me what you want. Blankets, sheets, pillow-cases, bedspreads, towels, table-cloths, napkins. Well, now, suppose I just look up what we have and report to you in fifteen minutes, say. How will that do? You give me the number of your phone, and I'll let you know styles and prices. Oh, it's no trouble whatever. I'll send the buyer around. She'll fix you up all right. You say you don't want very expensive things, just plain, good, substantial. All right. You stay where you are, 364 Morningside, you say. I'll call you up in about fifteen minutes."

Elsie hung up the receiver, and emerged into the outer world from the telephone booth, looking around her almost dazed. Life had gone so rapidly the last three hours that she seemed to have been whirled through things without any ability to stop or think. Now she suddenly realized she was tired and hungry.

She looked at her watch. It was twenty minutes to two. It seemed ages since she left her aunt's house for that tennis game after breakfast. In less than an hour the women would be at the house ready for work and she would have to be there. She must get something to eat.

The soda fountain offered a suggestion. She went over to investigate. Hot tomato bouillon, crisp crackers, and a sundae seemed a menu pleasant enough. She sat down to refresh herself while she awaited her telephone call.

AS SHE ate her lunch, Elsie's mind went back to the desolate house she had left, and gradually the thought took form, how pleasant it would be to set the dining-table and prepare a simple meal before she left.

She toyed idly with the idea, and put it from her many times, telling herself it would be impossible, for there was enough to do just to make things clean and get the beds ready for sleeping; and after she had finished her sundae she resolutely took out her pencil and note-book from her handbag, and began to figure out just what things she must have for the house and how much she could afford for each, that she might be ready to decide quickly when the prices were telephoned to her. This, of course, was absorbing for the time, and was barely done when the call came.

Five minutes later she emerged from the telephone booth well satisfied. Mr. Belknap had been very energetic and complete. He had arranged to have things delivered within two hours at the latest. He had discovered a number of bargains for her benefit, and he knew all about sizes and qualities, which she did not. His suggestions were valuable. She had the comfortable feeling that everything could be returned that was not satisfactory. He had told her of some wonderful values in eider-down quilts—of course only flowered sateen, but really neat and pretty, pink, blue, and yellow. He told her which blankets were warmest, said a dimity spread was good enough for daily use, and revealed to her ignorance the advantage of buying a dozen of the Turkish and huckaback towels on sale in the basement, and getting her table-cloths and napkins ready hemmed. He also suggested wash-rags, and promised to look up a few plain linen bureau-scarfs and a sideboard-cover to send with the rest. On the whole, she was very happy. There was half an hour before those women would be at the house. She had time to stop at the grocery and get soap, brooms, and a scrubbing-brush. That awful sink! What could she do with that? Wasn't it lye that Aunt Esther always used when the drain-pipes got stopped up? Yes, lye and boiling water.

Once in the store, she found a number of things that would help the work along—sand soap, silver-polish, floor-oil, a mop— It was remarkable how the list grew. For Elsie had been well brought up in ways of a household, and always had her regular duties with the daughters of the house. On Thursdays and Sundays when the cook went out she and Katherine and Bettina took turns in cooking the dinner, and each was proud of the specialities in the way of cookery in which she had learned to excel.

Now, as Elsie came to the other side of the store, where a genial-faced white-aproned butcher was tying up a luscious beef roast, she suddenly decided to yield to her desire to get dinner and leave it behind her in the lonesome house. There was a roast. It would be nothing at all to put that into the oven and roast it while she was doing other things. Then, when it was done, she could turn the gas low to keep it hot. And why not put some potatoes to roast beside it?

In a moment more she was bargaining for the roast and going excitedly around the store picking out various things: a head of lettuce, a few ripe tomatoes, a bottle of salad-oil, a can of corn, and another of beans to make succotash. How that dinner grew! Just as if she hadn't a whole house to clean in one short afternoon!

"How about some lovely canned pumpkin?" suggested the smiling storekeeper, thumping down a can with a great golden sphere represented on the decoration. "Like pumpkin pies? This is a new lot. Fine! Better try it."

Elsie hesitated. Pumpkin pies were her specialty. She could make delectable ones. But could she possibly get time to make pie-crust? Pies would be so nice and pleasant to have on hand, two or three of them for hungry men; and she had reached the stage in her game where she desired above all things to make a pleasant spot for those three forlorn ones of her family to come home to. She inquired whether they could get her some milk; and upon finding it possible she abandoned all thought of being judicious, and gave herself up to ordering. Eggs, sugar, flour, butter, lard, cinnamon, molasses, ginger, potatoes, bread, baking-powder—she would make some little biscuits too, if there was time—coffee. There seemed to be no end!

She suddenly discovered that she had but three minutes to get back to the house before her helpers arrived; and, seizing a bar of soap and a scrubbing-brush, she went away with the smiling assurance that her order would be sent up at once.

The two colored women entered the house in her wake with the air of two grim bronze censors who were about to discover for themselves what had long been an object of curiosity. They looked about alertly. Elsie was glad she had put a semblance of order into the rooms before she summoned assistance, and resolved not to let them go upstairs until she had first made some changes on the second floor.

"Now, we shall have to wash the dishes first and put this kitchen in order," she said, speaking firmly, as if disordered kitchens like that were quite common affairs.

"Laws! Mis' Elsie, they hev got things messed up, ain't they? I guess Rebecca wouldn't know the place. It's about a year since she went to work on the hill, ain't it?"

So Rebecca had gone to work on the hill. Elsie did not answer her interlocutor. She kept steadily on, giving directions. There was a mountain of work to be done, and she meant to have it done in the swiftest way.

"Just light all those gas-jets, and put on kettles of water to heat, and light the hot-water back. It will take a good deal of hot water. While we are waiting for it, suppose you sort out the dishes and get them stacked neatly so there will be room for the dishpans. Your daughter can empty out the water from the sink and get it ready to clean. Do you know how to fix that sink so it will work? I bought some lye."

"Yes, shur, honey, lye'll fetch it all right. It's de grease needs cuttin'. Lizzie, you git dat shovel, and dip out de water 'n' stuff in dat pail."

In a moment they were both interested in their work, and Elsie went upstairs to her room, slipped off her pretty dress, and donned an old gingham wrapper of her mother's which she found in a bureau drawer. Then she deliberately bundled up all the bedclothing from her father's and brothers' beds, tied them together for future reference, and carried them to the storeroom. By the time she had picked up the soiled clothes and hung up a few of the garments that were lying about, the grocery boy had come, and she went down to superintend the work below stairs. Dish-towels and dish-cloths were a problem; but she solved it by having a few old napkins washed out and hung over the gas-range to dry, and putting the dishes to drain out of very hot rinsing-water while they waited.

It is marvelous what three smart people can accomplish in a short space of time when one of them is a good leader. Elsie was not an old house-keeper; but she was a girl of great executive ability, and she had a definite idea of what she must do. She took the shortest cut she saw as a means to that end. The two servitors obeyed her commands with silence, respect, and growing interest. Before three o'clock every dish was washed and draining, and Lizzie had started to dry them while her mother wiped off the pantry and china-closet shelves, washed the tables, and scrubbed the kitchen floor.

Elsie meanwhile had been clearing out the débris from the sideboard drawers and consigning it all to two pasteboard boxes in the storeroom. Then, when the drawers were wiped out, they were ready for the knives and forks; and it seemed as if there was a clean spot from which to start.

As soon as the dishes were in their places Elsie set Lizzie and her mother to sweeping the worn rugs and oiling around the edges of the floor, the stairs and balustrade. Then with a look of almost guiltiness she stole into the kitchen and began her pies. There were difficulties to overcome in the form of no moulding-board and a misused rolling-pin with dents and creases all over it; but she managed to roll out three pretty creditable bottom crusts, and it took no time at all to mix the pumpkin, milk, eggs, sugar, spices, and molasses.

When she set the last pie triumphantly into the oven,

she realized that she was tired enough to cry. Her hands were fairly trembling in their haste, and her heart was beating wildly with the amount she had yet to accomplish before six o'clock. She had set that hour because she knew that shortly after that her father and brothers would arrive. She must have done by then all she would do that day, and be off. She felt now as if she were running a race. She ought to have telephoned Bettina that she was not going to that concert, and let her give her ticket to someone else; but there was no time to think of that. She fled to the other room, and was delighted to find that her assistants had both finished their tasks and were now at the upper hall. The house smelled pleasantly of soap and cedar oil. She glanced uneasily out of the front door. It was more than time for her order from the city to arrive. What if it should not come at all?

But she must not waste time thinking. She would get dinner ready as fast as possible before she had to open her parcels and dispose of their contents.

She selected the serving-dishes first, and set them in the warming-oven; it was the way her aunt had taught her at home. She washed the lettuce, prepared the tomatoes, and set them, three pretty plates, on the side-board with the bottle of salad-oil. She filled the sugar-bowl, and the salt and pepper cellars, opened her cans of corn and beans, washed her potatoes, and got the roast ready to be put into the oven; then the delivery-car arrived with the things, and everything had to be attended to at once. In the midst of opening her packages she almost forgot the roast; but, when it was safely in the oven, she hurried back to her bundles.

The women had finished the sweeping on the second floor, and were scouring the bathroom. She could hear their vigorous rubbings with sand soap on the sides of the bathtub and the old linoleum. She hurried the things out of their papers, rejoicing in their newness and whiteness. But there was no time to admire. Five minutes to a bed was all she ought to spare. Could she do it?

She spread on the sheets and blanket, smoothed a white coverlet over her father's bed, plumped the pillows into fresh cases, and tucked the pretty yellow sateen eider-down quilt in an artistic roll at the foot. What a difference it made! Then she seized one of the bureau-scarfs and whisked it upon the bureau. The room was a changed place.

With her heart swelling with pride and her arms filled with more sheets and blankets she went on to Eugene's room, and wrought the same magic change there. By this time the two women were scrubbing the third-story stairs, and would soon be up to Jack's room. She would wait to make up his bed and fix things till they came down.

She went down to the kitchen again, and found the pies gently simmering away, beginning to brown, and the roast sizzling contentedly. Then she dressed out the sideboard in its cover, and began to set the table. At once the whole house took on a comfortable, festive appearance, and the savory odors let out when she opened the oven door began creeping up even to the second and third stories, so that the two colored women felt the atmosphere, and talked in low tones about it.

"She's a right smart little girl," said the mother. "Reckon her mother'd be proud o' her."

"Did you take notice to the shoes she had on?" whispered her daughter. "Say, Ma, I'd like some like those. If she stays here and we work for her again, I'm agoin' to find out what she paid fer 'em."

When the table was set, Elsie ran out into the yard, and picked a handful of yellow roses from the straggling old bush in the yard, and put them into a vase in the centre of the table. They always had flowers of some kind on the dinner-table at Aunt Esther's. It gave the one little festive touch now that showed a woman had been at work trying to make things beautiful. The two helpers stopped on the stairs to admire.

"Say, now, ain't dat purty?" declared the mother, her eyes fixed on the bedecked table. "Say, ain't you handy, now? Flowahs suttinly do make a diffrunce. An' dem punkim pies suttinly do smell good."

Lizzie stood enviously watching the graceful girl as she flitted to and fro, putting the napkins around and arranging the spoons and forks.

Elsie set her helpers to cleaning out the back kitchen and making the back door more presentable while she went up to Jack's room. Somehow the making of that bed and the straightening of the old bureau and chiffonier there gave her more pleasure than what she had done on the other rooms, for Jack would always seem a child to her because he was nearer her own age.

She felt a trifle unhappy about making up the bed there on the floor, it looked so unfinished; but a swift survey of the old headboard and footboard showed her several reasons why Jack had abandoned them, for one leg was broken, and the main panel of the headboard was cracked from end to end. She returned to the low bed and made it as pretty as possible, with two plump white pillows at the head and the rosy eider-down quilt rolled artistically at the foot. She arranged the bureau-scarf, the prettiest one of all, and ran down to her room to bring up a little photograph of their mother framed in a silver frame, to set in front of the mirror.

After all, she looked around with dissatisfaction when it was finished. There was so much more that needed doing. There were no curtains whatever at the windows, no good cheer anywhere. But she had done her best for the present, and the woman was calling from below to say she had finished the back kitchen and must go home and get supper for her "man."

Elsie hurried down and paid her, taking a peep into the oven after they were gone. More savory odors floated out and filled the room invitingly. It was time to put in the potatoes and start the corn and beans to cooking. There was thickening to mix for the gravy, too; for she must have everything ready, and not be hindered at the last minute. It might be possible they would come home earlier than she expected, and she did not want to be in evidence when they arrived. This thought sent her flying to lock the front door and place the key under the mat as she had found it. They would be delayed for a minute to unlock the door, and she would have opportunity to slip unseen out of the back door and get away in case they came before she left.

She hurried in at the back door again. It was a quarter to six, and there was no time to waste. She cut the bread; got a plate of butter and a pitcher of fresh water; poured what milk was left into a pitcher; set out the pies to cool, putting one on the sideboard with three pie-plates beside it; took up the roast on its platter and set it in the warming-oven; made a beautiful bowl of rich brown gravy; and hurried upstairs to change her dress and obliterate all traces of her presence. Then with an anxious glance out of the window she stole quickly downstairs again; hung her hat and hand-bag on a hook in the back kitchen; left the doors unlatched conveniently for sudden flight; made the coffee; and took up her watch at the hall window, where she could command both the front and side streets.

It was ten minutes after six. She could hear the trolley-car coming in the distance. Her father might come on that, perhaps, and she ought to take the return one which would come down toward the city in another five minutes. She held her breath and watched anxiously. Somehow, now that her work was completed, she longed to stay and see its effect; but something half like shame withheld her. And, besides, she was by no means sure of her attitude toward her father and brothers. She had done this to-day for them, but was not prepared to have more obligations placed upon her. She wanted to think out the situation before she saw them again. She was not sure she wanted to see them at all, to have them know that she had done this.

She glanced swiftly back around the pretty table, across the tidy hall, into the shadowy depths of the living-room. It was still lonely and desolate, but nothing like what it had been when she came. She sniffed the luscious pie on the sideboard, thought of the white, warm beds upstairs, and was glad she had come. Then she looked back to her window, and saw a bus drawing up to the curb and her two brothers in working-garb getting out. They must be working over at the locomotive works.

She turned and fled to the kitchen. There was time to get the roast on the table. She flew to the table with the platter. A glance from the window showed her that her brothers were pausing to talk with one of the men who got out of the bus. She could bring the succotash and perhaps the gravy.

As she set down the gravy-boat, she saw they were turning to come in. One more trip with the potatoes! She could risk it, for they had to unlock the door yet; and they might not find the potatoes till after dinner if she didn't put them on the table. The coffee she could leave on the stove, for they would smell it.

As she paused to turn the gas-jet low under the

coffee-pot, she heard the key grate in the lock, and she fled precipitately out the back door into the laundry, closing it noiselessly behind her. She put on her hat with trembling hands. Picking up her bag she tiptoed down the back steps, pulling the door softly shut behind her, and slid around at the side under the old cherry tree where no one could see her. She could hear the trolley-car almost here now. She must hide until it had passed, and then run down the side street a few steps and cross over where she would not be noticed.

With dress held back she peeked cautiously around the corner of the kitchen. The trolley-car was stopping. Yes, her father was getting out. The conductor was steadying him as he went down the steps, as if he were old or sick. Ah! Did he stagger as he went out toward the curb? Her heart sank heavily. She watched with straining eyes. He was coming up the gravel walk, slowly, dejectedly, as if he did not care, with uneven steps, as if his mind were not on his walking.

With something like a sob in her throat the girl turned in panic, and fled noiselessly over the long, matted grass to the side street. She half expected them to come out after her, and walked almost half-way down the block before she dared look back to see that no one was following. Then simultaneously she heard the distant whir of the returning trolley-car, and realized that she must hasten if she would get back to the corner before it reached there. She crossed the street and hurried along, keeping well in the shadow of the hedges, and scarcely daring to look toward her home lest some one should be watching for her and recognize her.

But the house was very quiet. A sudden fear gripped her heart lest they should not discover the dinner before it grew cold; but the trolley was almost at hand. She could not linger to see. Then, as she turned to step out and signal the car, she saw a light flash up in the dining-room, and two—or was it three?—dim figures standing motionless in the middle of the room. Just that brief glimpse she caught as she climbed into the trolley and was whirled away cityward.

IT WAS Eugene who unlocked the front door and entered first. Jack lingered with a wistful look behind him at the sunset. Every night it was the same. Jack dreaded to enter that drear abode. He delayed the sight of the desolation as long as possible, and once inside the door put on a gruff, surly attitude toward everything, ate what supper he could get together in silence, made a frantic toilet in his cluttered room, and hastened away to spend the hours of leisure in whatever gayety presented itself in the dull little suburb.

Sometimes when Jack was feeling very lonely at thought of the house and the dreary life they lived, especially when there were low gray clouds in the west and there was no sunset, he would think of his mother's coffin there in the parlor as it had been five years ago. He could press his eyelids and bring back the white, still features and the sweet young look that was not she, but some bright thing related to her and reminding of her, so far, so very far away! At such times Jack was fairly savage, and often went off without his supper.

To-night Eugene halted as he reached the hallway,

hesitating in the dusk, as if something imperceptible had put forth an unseen hand and stopped him. It was too near dark in the house to tell what had happened, but he knew at once by all his senses that something had. Things did not assert themselves in the same way as they usually did. The sense of confusion was gone. The dusty, musty smell had departed. He did not become aware at once of how much everything needed cleaning up. He felt a sudden calm; he might almost have called it peace if he had been analyzing it. And, speaking of smells, what mingling of delicious savoriness was this that greeted his famished senses? Not coffee with an aroma like that! They made coffee for themselves, and it never sent forth fragrance of such a sort. Could his father have come home first and had an unusual spirit of unselfishness? The odor began to differentiate itself. Was that roasting meat? When had they had a roast? It suggested Christmas and other days of long ago. But that other spicy fragrance? What was it? Newly baked bread? Gingerbread? What? He could not tell, but something sweet and succulent and toothsome that recalled far-distant days of festivity.

And last his faltering mind took in the sense of a sweet foreign influence, he might almost think a presence, so much so that he stood still and held his breath to listen for a stir of garments, or a voice to speak. But the only real sound that came was the contented bubbling of the coffee in the kitchen. Without any reason he felt sure that, whatever presence was or had been about, it was not his father. Something sweet and tender and brooding was in the atmosphere, and how he knew all this without even putting it into thoughts he could not have told. It just entered his consciousness like the joy of a day that one has expected to be grim and gray, and suddenly the sun bursts through and glorifies everything. So stood

Eugene Hathaway in the doorway of his home and took in the difference.

He stood still till Jack, with his head turned to get the last glimpse of crimson in the west, ran full into him and halted with an exclamation that denoted shock rather than any other emotion. Jack's highly strung temperament was always keyed up to the highest pitch when he entered the door of his home, he dreaded it so.

Then there happened to him, too, that wonderful sense of something new, the perception of cleanliness and comfort, of something good to eat and good cheer; and he too stepped in beside his brother, and stopped looking around in the gloaming, as though in a mood of thoughtlessness he had stepped unaware into a sanctuary and found the people worshipping. He stood abashed, and looked around.

The car had stopped, and their father's step was heard uncertainly, aimlessly coming up the gravel walk before they bestirred themselves. It was Eugene who made the first move into the strangeness and lighted up. Then both stepped forward with a curious look about them as if they were exploring new regions, on into the hominess of the dining-room where that delicious dinner sat inviting them to eat!

Clean table-cloth! Napkins! Clean dishes! A glass salt-cellar! These were things that spoke eloquently of the newness. A great roast, steaming hot, and brown as velvet! Gravy, real gravy! Steaming, too. Potatoes cracking open, and ah! that delicious spicy sweetness, more definite now and more alluring! It was Jack who first discovered the pie, and tiptoed over to stoop down and smell again, as if he might scare it away if he did not walk lightly. They stood and gazed in silence, gazed again as famished travellers sometimes dream of all the good things they would like to eat, and see them in mirage; so they feasted their eyes upon it, as on something that might vanish in a moment.

It was Jack again who, feeling that sense of a foreign presence, stole into the kitchen to investigate, and came back with awe in his young face, and stood once more gazing.

The father found them so when he stepped into the lighted dining-room, his senses, less alert than his sons', and noticed nothing till he came full into the doorway. Then he drew back startled, passed his hand across his eyes, and looked again. Looked, and turned his head aside, and gave a great gasp like a sob. Turned back and gazed, shamedly, first at one son and then the other; saw they knew no more than he how this miracle had come to pass; then suddenly dropped into a chair, burying his face in his hands, with another gasp like a sob. The table had not looked so since his wife died, those five long years ago. His body shook with dry, inarticulate sobs. His sons looked at him and at each other, and were speechless. There were no words to meet the occasion. They knew without words what those sobs meant. It was the first glimpse they had had into their father's soul since they were little lads.

But the embarrassment of the moment aroused Jack to action, and dismissed the sudden hush and awe that had come over his young spirit.

"Well, I say, let's eat it, anyway! It's here, and it's getting cold. It was evidently meant to eat. That is, if it's real. I'm not sure, but I mean to make a stab at trying it. Who's going to carve! Here, you, Dad, sit up there at the head of the table, and carve! I'm hungry as a bear. We had spoiled fish at the restaurant at the works to-day, and I couldn't eat a mouthful for the smell of it. Get on to your job, Dad, and slice her down."

But the man lifted his head, and shook it helplessly.

There were tears in his eyes and trickling down the furrows in his cheeks. They understood that he did not feel himself worthy to divide that banquet. They turned away, and sat down with more respect for him than they had felt for years. They would not look upon his shame and sorrow. It touched them that he should feel as he did.

But they were young, and hungry, and the food was good. So Eugene went to the head, and cut the meat in an awkward way, and served it on the plates; and Jack went out to the kitchen, and brought in the coffee-pot. They made their father draw up his chair, trying in sudden tenderness to extend a large cordiality which they had not felt for him of late. His breath was strong of liquor, but it had not affected him much. They had ceased to reproach him or to reason with him. It was useless. Let him to his way, and they would go theirs, endure the little contact necessary, and see that it was the least possible.

But now to-night in the strange new surroundings, with the delicious meal before them, they treated him as they might have treated a naughty child who was sorry and wanted to be comforted. And so they heaped his plate with good things, and made him sit up to the table. But he could not eat. He would sit and look at his plate, and try to take a mouthful; and then he would lay down his fork, still with the delicate bit of roast beef upon it, and say,

"Did you do it, Jack?"

"No, Dad, I just got home."

"Did you do it, Gene? You never liked to cook. You couldn't cook like this."

"No, Dad, I didn't do it. I just got home, too. We just came in the door as your car came."

"There's only one could cook like this!" the father

said, and bowed his head in his hands, so that they had to cheer him up again to make him eat.

They could see what he was thinking. In his bewilderment superstition had taken hold upon him. He was going back to the days that were past. The food was miraculous to him. He could not eat it. He felt himself unworthy.

And when at last they had made him eat a little, and the comforting food had warmed his body and strengthened him, he sat and looked about on the rooms and at the table in a daze of wonder and sorrow.

They finished that pie thoroughly. The father ate only one small piece. The two boys ate all the rest, and easily. They could have demolished the other two, possibly, if they had discovered them in time. But at last they sat back satisfied.

"Some dinner!" approved Jack as he folded his napkin reverently, and carefully scraped all the crumbs from the table-cloth upon his plate. "Say, old boy, keep the table looking this way awhile! Let's clear it off, and wash up the dishes, and get things in shape for tomorrow. There's meat enough for a good spread, and succotash, too," peering into the dish. "We'll have a regular high-class Sunday dinner without much work. Come on; let's tote the things out and wash up."

When they turned up the light in the kitchen they were amazed to find that the cleanliness and order had penetrated there too. The disgusting flood in the sink had vanished, also the smell belonging thereto. The range was washed clean, and the shelves were all in order. The kitchen table was arranged with the dishpans for washing the dishes, and there appeared to be something clean to wipe them with. A scratching at the laundry door led them to open it for the cat, which walked in lean and gaunt, sniffing the air offendedly. All this prosperity, and she not asked to share it? Her eyes fairly blazed with the indignity, but Jack had time to notice the order in the laundry before he shut the door behind her and came back to give her some scraps of beef and the potato-skins. She was not a dainty cat. Her experience had taught her better. This was a banquet for her.

The young men tidied up the supper-table, put away the food, and washed the dishes, for the most part in silence. But, when they found the pumpkin pies set up on the dresser shelf to cool, they looked at each other; and a great question was in their eyes.

"Say, you don't suppose Elsie could have done it," Jack voiced the thought at last.

"No chance!" said Eugene contemptuously. "She's too much of a fine lady. I don't suppose she ever sees the inside of a kitchen. How could she make a pumpkin pie? Besides, she wouldn't lift one of her dainty fingers for us. We're only poor relations. The last time I saw her she was all dolled up like a plush horse. She probably spends all her time out of school learning how to bob her hair a new way. And what would she do it for?"

Sure enough. That was a poser. Jack had been fond of Elsie but he couldn't answer that.

"Well, who *could* have, then?" he said at last after he had wiped the three cups and set them on the shelf.

"Search me! I give up. It does seem uncanny."

"Rebecca couldn't do it. She never cooked like that."

"Not on your life she couldn't unless she's met with a change of heart and hand."

"Well, how do you explain it?" insisted Jack.

"I don't explain it," said Eugene. "Just take it as it is. Think it just happened."

"I wish it would happen again!" sighed Jack, turning thoughtfully toward the door and looking into the pleasant dining-room, his eyes resting on the flowers in the middle of the table.

"Flowers, too! Gee! It's queer!" he soliloquized.

"What you going to do to-night, Jack? Going to the movies?"

"I was," said Jack uninterestedly, "but I don't know's I will to-night. It's so pleasant here I'd like to enjoy it while it lasts. It won't take long for it to get back the way it was. Get onto that hall? I haven't seen that closet door shut for two years. And somebody's mended the newel. I say, old boy, why didn't we ever think to do that?"

"H'm! Don't know. Didn't seem worth while, I guess, there was so much else the matter. Say, it looks nice, don't it? I s'pose we might fix up a little now and then ourselves but I never have time. I've gotta date to-night. Ought to be gone by now. What time is it?"

He looked at his watch.

"Good-night, kid, did you know it was almost nine o'clock? No use going now. Well, I wouldn't have believed it was so late. We must have been almost two hours eating our supper. Some banquet, eh?"

"Yes, some banquet!" re-echoed the younger brother. "Well, what say we have some music?" He strolled toward the long-neglected piano, and opened it. Sitting down, he began to play a modern popular piece and to chant in a deep, not unmusical bass, some unintelligible words, whose main object seemed to be to crowd into the rhythm with remarkable celerity.

The father dozed in his chair; waked, looked around again with tears in his eyes; dozed again dreaming of his dead wife; and the boys sang on for some time.

At last Jack closed the piano and got up. He couldn't play much but chords; but he bluffed the rest, and really managed to get quite a bit of pleasure out of it.

"Gee!" he said wistfully, yawning and looking at his

watch. "Gee! I wish we had a sister or something in the house! Now I s'pose we've to crawl up to that old hole and get some sleep. I've a notion to lie here on the floor to-night. I get a nightmare up in my room sometimes just thinking how it looks."

"Don't turn on the light," suggested his brother, "then you can't see."

"H'm! You don't know what you're talking about. I couldn't find the bed without a light; the floor's knee-deep with truck. Well, so-long! I'm going to hit the hay. All this excitement's bad for a working man."

Jack slowly, reluctantly ascended the stairs, putting his hand affectionately on the old newel. The top quivered under his grasp, toppled an instant, and fell crashing to the floor.

As if he had hurt a child, the boy hastened back, picked it up, examined the difficulty, hunted up the hammer which he remembered to have seen on the pantry shelf, and drove the nails securely into place again. Then he went upstairs without more ado.

EUGENE took the evening paper from his coatpocket, and settled down to read a few minutes, but it was not quiet overhead. Jack's footsteps had paused for a moment on the upper landing with that queer, indefinable breathlessness that both boys had felt when they first entered the house that evening, and then started excitedly from room to room on the second floor. The noisy footsteps pounded up the third-story stairs, and there was a moment's quiet, a long moment during which Eugene began to read the athletic scores of the day. Suddenly Jack's feet were heard again clattering down the stairs.

"Say, Gene! Come up here!" he shouted excitedly before he had reached the second-story landing. There was something in his tone that brought his brother up three steps at a time.

It was to the bathroom shining in its purity that Jack first led his brother. The tub white as enamel could be, the faucets bright, the soap dish immaculate, the floor so clean the pattern of the old linoleum could be seen again, and the towel-racks literally overflowing with white, luxurious towels!

It was at those towels that the brothers gazed longest, reaching out to feel of them, unfolding one to see its length and breadth. They had so long used little, inadequate affairs of doubtful character that a bath had become an unpleasant necessity rather than a pleasure.

"Some class!" murmured Eugene rapturously. "I believe I'll take a bath! Say, I'd like to know who the fairy is that has touched this house with her magic wand while we were away."

"Just wait till you see!" ejaculated Jack, gripping his brother's shoulder and whirling him about face.

Eugene stood in his own room doorway, and looked about dazed. The clean white bed, the dainty bureau-scarf, the cleared-up appearance, were almost unbelievable. Something softening came over his face, which was inclined to be cynical.

"Good-night!" he said at last softly. "I guess I'll go to bed. But I'll have to take a bath before I get into that bed. I wonder if I've got any clean pajamas. Say, Jack, did that laundry come? I wonder."

But Jack kept a firm grip on his shoulder, and marched him on to see the rest of the house.

"Third story, too?" asked Gene, surprised as Jack pushed him toward the stairs after a glimpse of his father's room. "Well, there must have been a fairy godmother along, too, to get all this done in one day. I think it would take several wands working double time to accomplish so much. It looked like a pretty hopeless dump to me when I left here this morning. I was thinking as I left the house that I'd like to touch a match to it and burn the whole thing up and begin again. It certainly was a mess!"

"Some mess! Especially my dump!" assented Jack as he threw his own door wide open and waved his brother inside.

"Some change I should say!"

Gene's eyes travelled all about, and halted at his mother's picture on the bureau. He went over and stood before it, looking long and earnestly. Then he spoke, and his voice was husky and unnatural.

"Things would 'a' been different if she'd lived, kid," he said half embarrassedly.

"Sure!" agreed Jack in a faint, shy tone, turning his back and looking out of the window.

"Do you remember what a wonderful woman she was, kid?"

"Sure, I do!" came the voice from the window with a little tremble to it.

The older brother sighed, and turned to go downstairs.

"Gee! 'twould be great if she could come back! Things like this all the time! And she here every night when we came home!" he said, unexpectedly voicing the wistfulness that was in both their minds.

"Wouldn't it, though?" Jack sauntered down behind his brother as though he could not quite give up the subject, but neither spoke of it again. Gene pushed Elsie's door open, and glanced in.

"Nothing doing in there! Fairy godmother doesn't approve of her!" declared Jack facetiously.

Gene brought it shut with a bang, and sighed heavily. The room they had by common consent tried to keep as it had been for the sake of the sister whom it belonged—for the sake of having some shrine in the house whereat to worship—looked bare and desolate beside the other rooms now. He wanted to shut it away in its dust and emptiness and forget it.

"Wake Dad up and bring him up here!" he commanded. "I'm going to light the hot-water back, and have a bath!"

What with the excitement and the splashing and the search for clean laundry it was late, after all, before the brothers were ready for those clean white beds that drew them so invitingly.

Just as Jack was about to go up to his room at last, they were both drawn by some occult power toward their father's open door to see what had become of him. They found him asleep on his knees before the bed, with their mother's old wrapper hugged close in his arms and traces of tears on his face.

Tenderly, with unaccustomed hands and words that sounded strangely on their young lips, they roused him and made him go to bed. They crept awesomely into their own beautifully clean beds, and lay down, handling the covers carefully as though these might be harmed with rougher touch. And then they lay with crowding thoughts upon their hearts. They had not been so stirred since their mother died. They felt her presence had somehow come back again to bless them. It may be that the thankfulness of their hearts as they put their heads upon those clean pillows, and sighed contentedly, was something akin to prayer.

The whole thing was so mysterious, so wholly unexplainable by any of the common surroundings and circumstances of their lives, that they could in no wise settle on an explanation; and there was nothing else but Providence to lay it to. They had never thought much about Providence. They had scarcely thought they believed in higher powers any more. It wasn't exactly the thing to do in the world in which they moved.

There was not an aunt in the whole connection who would have done this for the house and them, no, not even for the sweet morsel of giving them a rebuke. There was not a devoted old servant; for Rebecca had been the only servant they had had for years, and Rebecca never had a knack of making things look tidy, nor could she cook like that.

Besides, there were those wonderful soft blankets, the new white spreads, the sheets, the towels. Who, *who* would spend money for such things for them? They turned back the spread in the dark, and touched lightly the soft wool of the blanket, to make sure it was still there. They passed wondering hands again over the smoothness of the sheets. Would the mystery ever be explained? Would they perhaps find it was some practical joke? Or, worse still, a terrible mistake? Some one had got the wrong house and done all this? How could it be? Yet there was no other reasonable explanation.

The older man, moaning in his room, was talking to his dead wife; telling her how he had treated her, how dear and wise she had been to him, and how he had rewarded her with sorrow. He pleaded with her to come back once more, just to touch him and say she forgave.

The boys, listening in the darkness and the stillness of the house, found their own lashes were wet in spite of themselves. It seemed to them that their mother had just died; yet she was there in the front room with their father, receiving her due from him at last. It half reconciled them to their father to hear him make this late reparation. It stirred their souls to the depths, and somehow brought up things that they themselves had done which would have distressed their mother. In that still hour in those comfortable beds some things they had been contemplating for themselves fell away from them, and a cleaner, truer purpose half rose in their hearts for the future.

And at last they fell into a clean, untroubled sleep, with a sense as of a hand tenderly comforting them.

WHEN Elsie got into the trolley at her father's corner and sank down into a seat, she was suddenly overcome with an unutterable weariness. She did not remember ever to have been so tired before. Her limbs trembled, and even her fingers trembled as she tried to take her fare out of her purse. It seemed as though her heart was on a gallop and she could not keep up with it. She wanted to cry out to it to stop and let her get her breath, and she wanted to throw herself down on the seat and weep. It was hard to keep the tears back, and she knew her lips must be visibly trembling. She could not understand this sudden collapse.

She put her purse into her bag and leaned her head against the window, closing her eyes and trying to get steady control of herself. Those last few minutes, slipping out of the house like a thief, running away from her brothers and her own father, watching her father go uncertainly up the walk, had been too much for her. She had been keyed up all day for this climax, and now that it was over and she was speeding away from the scene of her activities, her mind could not stop.

It suddenly began to seem all wrong for her to be going away. Her place was back there in that miserable house, trying to make it pleasant for those to whom she had been given when she came into the world. Those three desolate men, for whom she had been laboring all day as a sort of amusement for herself, had a claim upon her that no other three people in the whole world had. She had never thought of it in that way before. She had not even thought of it while she had been trying to make the house habitable for them. She had only looked upon it as a charitable incident in her full and happy life. Now it suddenly took on proportions that overwhelmed her, and she was physically too tired to reason or to combat them. The tears came into her eyes, with torrents threatening. In vain she dabbed at the edges of her lashes to remove a sudden glistening; in vain she pressed her upper lip with her finger; in vain she opened her eyes and sat up straight, winking fast to remind herself that people were about her and she must not cry. Two tears welled up and rolled flashing down her cheeks before she could think, and she turned her head sharply toward the window to hide them and got out her handkerchief to wipe them away. She stared hard out of the window, and kept her eyes wide to prevent more tears; and, as she looked into the window-glass, she became aware of a face behind her, oddly, hauntingly familiar which gave one keen, sympathetic glance and turned away as if he would not watch what he could not but see she wished to hide.

She conquered her tears presently, but continued to stare out of the window and could see the reflection of the young man who had happened to be looking that way when her tears fell. He had a kindly expression, pleasant firm lips. Where had she seen him before and why did his face remind her of something unpleasant?

He did not keep looking at her curiously as some men might have done. She thanked him in her heart for that.

She did not know that he had stood within the shadow of the great willow-tree across the corner from her father's house, waiting for this car, when she stole furtively to the back door and ran down the street; nor did she know that he had recognized her at once as the pretty dancer of the evening before and wondered, for she did not look as if she belonged to a dejected, lonely home like that. The manner of her egress from the house, if she had but known it, had been peculiar enough to arouse anyone's curiosity, and, when there were added to this her weary looks and the tears, he certainly had items enough to make the situation interesting.

Cameron Stewart had been out to Morningside to call on an old friend of his mother's before taking his train and he had been standing at that corner when the young men arrived and had seen the man get off the up car and go into the house none too steadily. Was that the burden the girl carried? And if so, what relation did she sustain to him and to the two younger men in working clothes who had entered the house just as the girl left it? Could she by any chance be a daughter? Professor Bowen had spoken only of a rich uncle.

He tried to forget the girl across the aisle, and to tell himself that she was nothing but a stranger to him, that he had no business to be prying even with his thoughts into her affairs; but, try as he would, the sweet face and the fresh content of the girl he had seen the evening before kept coming to him, in sharp contrast with the weary young face leaning against the window now with closed eyes and a tired droop to the lips. Curious that he could feel such interest in her now when he had despised her so thoroughly last night. But this was an entirely different view of her. In spite of his best efforts he was interested and worried about that girl to such a degree that he forgot to get off his car at the station and had to hurry away with a last wistful glance in her direction and walk back three blocks. He had half a mind to stay on the car and see where she went, but chided himself severely for the thought. It was almost time for his train, and what business had he to run after an unknown girl just because he felt sorry for her?

When Elsie reached her aunt's house, she found the family quite worked up about her absence. They had delayed dinner for her, and had telephoned to every possible place they could think of to find out where she was. There was company to dinner, and no time for explanations. One of Bettina's friends had brought a college friend to see the girls, and the young men had been delighted to accept the eager invitation to stay to dinner. Elsie hurried upstairs to make a hasty toilet, both sorry and glad for the company. She felt too weary and absorbed to arouse herself to talk small nothings now, but at least she would not have to go into details of explanation as she might have had to do if none but the family were there.

"Where on earth have you been, child?" said her aunt, hurrying in as Elsie came down. "I've been worried sick about you. You missed the symphony concert, and you wanted to hear it so much."

"I've been out to Morningside, Aunt Esther," she said, trying to speak brightly. "I'm sorry about the concert, but I just couldn't come back any sooner. I found some things that had to be done."

"At Morningside all day!" exclaimed her aunt in dismay. "But really, Elsie, you shouldn't do that, you know. It is utterly uncalled for. There is a servant paid to look after things out there, and you have your own life to live. It was too bad for you to miss the concert."

Elsie was glad that the others came about her and she had to be introduced to the young men. She did not feel like combating her aunt just now, and somehow that good woman's point of view seemed utterly out of focus with the girl's present mood. For the first time since she had come to live with her aunt such remarks about her father's home grated upon her. That talk about her living her own life sounded utterly selfish and cruel. *Did* she have her own life to live in that sense? Some long-forgotten words rushed to her memory; where had she heard them? "For none of us liveth to himself." Was it true? What did it mean? Hadn't she been living to herself? Wasn't that what Aunt Esther was trying to have her do? Out of kindness and love for her, of course; but still didn't it amount to the same thing? Aunt Esther of course hated Elsie's father because he had married her younger sister, and, according to Aunt Esther, had broken her heart. She also hated the boys because they were boys, and might be expected to follow in the footsteps of their father. She had taken Elsie away from it all. That was what Elsie had often heard her tell the other aunts and cousins and, until to-night, had always felt a deep gratitude to Aunt Esther for having taken her. Each visit to her old home had confirmed her in that gratitude. But now for the first time she began to see another side to such remarks. She began to wonder whether perhaps Aunt Esther had really done the very best thing for her that she could have done.

There was not much time for these thoughts. Another young man, a friend of Katharine's arrived; and almost at once they sat down to dinner. The stranger was assigned to Elsie and she found her hands entirely full to keep up with his merry repartee. She was obliged to summon all her powers to the task, and once, when Katharine was telling some story that engaged the attention of the entire table, she leaned back wearily in her chair with relief; but her aunt noticed her, and spoke as soon as there was opportunity.

"Elsie, you are looking pale and tired. You shouldn't have tired yourself all out going over your old things. It really isn't worth while. It would have been much better for you to have just given the name of that book you wanted to the book-store, and asked them to get you a copy, than for you to travel away out there and wear yourself to a frazzle."

With a bright spot of color on each cheek Elsie rallied again, trying to laugh and hide the tendency to burst into tears that seemed to be returning upon her. It was harder than anything she had done all day to sit there and make small talk, and be wondering the while whether her father and brothers ate the dinner before it was cold, whether they found the coffee-pot in time, whether the gravy had been salted enough, and whether they had cared at all. Would they go upstairs before they ate supper, and discover the changes she had made there? If they did, the supper would surely be cold before they ate it; and that would be such a pity.

It was wonderful how that house out at Morningside had taken a hold upon her thoughts, and how many times she had to bring her mind back with a jerk to the conversation she was trying to carry on.

The evening had been terribly long. They had insisted upon her playing for them; then she had to accompany Bettina when she sang; and then they all sang. It seemed as though the hours stretched out interminably. But at last it was over; her aunt had kissed her good-night; and somehow she got through all the chatter with her cousins, listening half-heartedly to "And he said," and "He was awfully pleased," and "Don't you think he's handsome, Elsie," and so on, until they finally confessed to being sleepy and left her to herself.

She crept into bed thankfully; yet, even as she turned back the coverings of her comfortable bed she felt a pang when she remembered those awful beds she had encountered that morning; and, when she put her head down on the pillow and shut her eyes, she had to wonder again what her brothers and father had said. Were they pleased or angry at having the house changed? Did they like the supper? Did they suspect who had done it? A kind of shame burned in her cheeks in the dark, as she reflected that they would have no reason whatever from her own actions during the past five years even to think of herself in connection with it.

Then, as she turned over and expected to float off to sleep on the wings of her great weariness, there came a vision of her own old room, a dusty dreary vision; an empty room, but a shrine for her! Somehow it seemed to be stretching out its weird, dusty hands to her over the miles of city that separated them, and to be calling to her to come and make it live again and be a centre for that desolate home. A home without a woman! What a place it was! It was almost worse than a home without a man, and Elsie had always thought that would be most stupid and dull. But a home without a woman was no home at all; she had seen that to-day. It was a shell with the spirit gone. And there was no woman but herself to take that place, bring that home to life again, and make it what it ought to be for those three men.

True, in a few years, perhaps soon, one of the boys might marry and bring home a wife; but it was utterly unlikely that any woman would want to be brought home to a place like that. She would more than likely insist that she have a new home of her own; and she would be entirely justified in it. She would have no obligation to make that home live again. Only the daughter of the house had the obligation upon her to do that. Why had that obligation never appeared to her before? Why had she been content to live here in peace and luxury and forget these who were her own blood? Why did she see things differently now? Nothing was changed from what it had been this morning when she left the house. She had known that things out there were dreary. She had been perfectly happy then to let them be so and live her own life; what had made the difference? Why could she not get back that calm, philosophical way of looking at life, feeling that, as Aunt Esther had said, she had her own life to live?

She had no desire to have her eyes opened in this way. She would have liked to close them again and go back to comfortable living. She pulled the bed-clothes over her head, and tried to shut out the sight of the dining-room window with that sudden light, and the three dark figures standing about as at a sacrament, just before the trolley-car took her away from it all. She got up and bathed her head with cologne, took a drink of water, and tried to compose herself to sleep again; but all the while the thoughts were racing through her mind, the questions pouring in upon her heart that had never asked themselves of her before. Questions of right and wrong. Deep, solemn questions, as if she were being arraigned before a throne of justice. And underneath, like an eager, other soul that saw beyond selfishness, was running a wonder as to how they had taken her surprise, and what would happen next?

She dreaded her aunt's questioning in the morning, which she knew was sure to come. She dreaded the sneers and jokes of her cousins when they had time to take in that she had actually stayed away from the symphony concert to clear up a house and make pies. She dreaded most of all to face her real self on the morrow when she should be rested and know what verdict her soul had rendered to itself for all that she had done and had left undone for the past five years.

And so at last she slept.

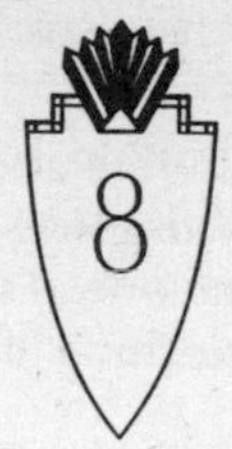

ELSIE kept her own counsel most of the week. She avoided discussions with her aunt concerning Morningside, and she managed to turn the conversations away from the symphony concert whenever an approach to it threatened, so that her cousins asked no more unpleasant questions.

But, when a friend telephoned Friday evening and asked her to go to the university play Saturday afternoon, she declined on the plea that she had another engagement; and Bettina, overhearing, grew unmercifully curious, and began begging her to go to a famous moving-picture play with them Saturday afternoon. She evaded Bettina successfully, but Saturday morning Halsey Kennedy drove up in his big motor-car, and invited all three girls to go on an all-day trip with himself and a friend. Of course Elsie's negative brought a torrent of exclamations and coaxings upon her, and Katharine and Bettina finally went off in a huff with the deeply disappointed young men.

It was a little hard for Elsie, standing in the door watching them depart, to know that she might have had the front seat and the exclusive attention of Halsy Kennedy for the day if she had gone. The task she had set herself looked like a dismal one as she turned away from the brightness of the morning and went upstairs to prepare for it.

She soon came down, however, in a street suit with a large neat bundle in her arms, and hurried away to the trolley-car, thankful that her aunt had already gone to an early committee meeting of the Civic Section of the Woman's Club, and therefore could not protest.

She did not take a book along this time. There were things to think over and decide, things that somehow she had been unable to decide in her aunt's house.

She was the same girl, sitting in the trolley-car taking the same trip she had taken the week before; and yet there was about her an air of purposeful strength that had not been there before. This girl now was not merely a creature of beauty enjoying life. She looked as though her eyes had been opened and her ears had heard the call to duty. There was a set about her pretty lips that did not speak of self-indulgence and a gleam in her pleasant eyes that made one feel that here was a girl who would accomplish something in life.

She left the trolley-car before she reached her father's house. She desired to approach from the side street and reconnoitre. The fact that she had heard nothing from her father during the week made her reasonably sure that he had not guessed that it was she who had made the mysterious visit last week. Still, she wished to remain unknown for a little while longer; so she walked around by the way of the store, left an order, and came back to the house by way of the side street, approaching the back door whence she had fled in the dusk of the evening.

All was quiet about the house. The back door was closed and locked. A furtive glance at the windows revealed no sign of anyone in the house. She went up to the front door. Some one had picked up the papers and straightened the old chairs. One chair, the most dilapidated of all, had disappeared. Perhaps her example had incited a desire to keep things looking better. The leaves had been raked up about the door, and things outside did not look quite so forlorn, although there was plenty yet to be done. The lower step was weaker and more wabbly than ever.

The day was warm for that time of year, and the gaunt cat had folded herself neatly together on the railing of the porch in the sun, her paws doubled closely, eyes like two tailored button-holes set slantwise in the lapels of a coat. A very common, cold little pussy, seeking to get warm in the sun, asking little of the world and receiving less.

The key was under the mat, and Elsie looked anxiously about as she entered to see whether the good cheer she had left behind last week had remained.

Yes, everything was in order, as if great pains had been taken to leave it so. The closet door was closed, and no coats or hats were about. Even the papers were piled together under the table, and there had been a rude attempt to sweep up the dust; for she could see the marks of the broom in long dabbling sweeps, alternating with the places where the broom had not touched. Something queer and sweet leaped in her breast at the sight of that. It was a little message from the three to say that they had liked what she had done.

A glimpse into the dining-room and kitchen showed awkward attempts to clean up and to keep things looking as she had left them. The tears sprang unbidden to her eyes as she realized this.

Upstairs the rooms had been kept very tidy, and the beds were spread up bunglingly with brave attempts to make them smooth.

With her heart somehow suddenly light and happy Elsie slipped into the little cotton gown and apron she had brought along, and ran downstairs. She had decided to bake more pies and make some cookies and gingerbread. These were things that would last a few days and not deteriorate. She had copied from her aunt's cookbook several recipes for her use, and now she set about getting things into order for the day.

She had brought with her some simple muslin curtains which she had bought during the week. She proceeded to put them up while she waited for the things to come from the store.

It did not take long to do it and to smooth out the wrinkles from the man-made beds; then she was ready for her baking.

If the young man who had asked her to go in an automobile with him, and the friend who wanted her to go to the play, and the cousins who could not understand why she had chosen to stay at home, could have seen her with bright eyes and rosy cheeks flying around that kitchen for the next few hours, they would have stared in amazement. When she finally slipped out of the door at five minutes after six, not risking another car, lest she should be caught, she left behind her a row of pies, a big bowl of cookies, two tins of gingerbread, and a nicely cooked dinner; and her heart was very light and happy as she sank into her seat in the trolley. She knew she was going to meet with reproaches when she got back to Aunt Esther's, but she didn't care; she had done what she thought was right, and she never felt happier in her life.

For three weeks Elsie kept up her pilgrimages, growing more and more deeply interested in the household of Morningside, finding extra little things to do for them, leaving touches of beauty and comfort behind her, and gradually obliterating the traces of desolation.

The weeks were not filled with roses altogether, for her path was conscientiously strewn with thorns of advice and protest by her aunt and cousins; and she found it necessary to get up early and slip away before breakfast that third Saturday, lest she be prevented entirely.

The day had gone well, and she was singing a little song as she worked. It was doughnuts she had elected to fry that afternoon, and everything was coming on finely. The dinner was well started; a big pan of biscuits was cooling in the pantry, a whole platterful of doughnuts well sprinkled with powdered sugar was on the kitchen table; and she was just cutting out another lot of them for frying when suddenly she became aware that she was not alone in the room! With that stealthy alertness we have when we become conscious of another presence Elsie looked up, and there in the pantry door stood both her brothers, their faces filled with wonder and delight, looking at her as if they could not believe that she was real.

She dropped the dough she was just lifting from the moulding-board, and clasped her hands with a little startled cry. She was surprised to find a tightening of joy around her heart. She stood for a second reading the surprise and pleasure in their faces; and then she sprang forward toward them, her arms outstretched, just as she used to do when she was a little bit of a girl.

Startled, abashed, the two great fellows braced themselves for her coming, and, flinging their arms about her, lifted their sister from her feet, and held her so between them for a moment, with a look almost of adoration in their faces.

The girl's heart leaped up unexpectedly, and she felt a great wave of love for them sweep over her. After all, they were her own brothers; and how strong and splendid they seemed, lifting her in this way as if she were a feather! She put an arm around each, and kissed first one and then the other, half laughing, half ashamed at the surge of emotion within her.

"Say, kid, this is great!" burst forth Jack. "We couldn't make out who was the fairy; so we thought we'd steal a march on her, whoever she was."

They had put her upon her feet, but stood each side of her, looking down from their young height with pride and tenderness, as if they could hardly believe they had her, as if it were too good to be true.

"It was wonderful!" said Gene; "but we didn't think it was you. We didn't suppose you could cook like that—that is, we didn't suppose you had time for such things. We—" He stopped, realizing that he was showing her just what kind of an opinion he had had of her.

But she nestled her head against his shoulder, lovingly, "You thought I was a feather-brained, giddy little girl who couldn't do a single sensible thing; and you thought, anyhow, that I didn't care a cent for you. I begin to see that you had good reason to think so, too. But I never understood; really I didn't! I didn't realize that you needed me—at least, you needed some one."

"That's it, we needed you," said Gene drawing his arm closer around her, and taking her little floury hand in his.

"Here! Let me in on this!" cried Jack, throwing his big arms around the two of them and almost smothering his sister.

Thus in a merry scrimmage the moment of their meeting was tided over, and suddenly the kettle of fat on the stove asserted itself.

"Oh, my doughnuts!" screamed Elsie, rushing back to see the three fat floaters already turning very dark indeed.

"Doughnuts!" said Jack. "That's what we smelled! Gee! This is great! Can I have one now?"

"Take all you want!" said Elsie grandly, her heart rejoicing in the ability to give.

They ate doughnuts, and helped her to make more; and, while it all was going on they were stealing shy looks at one another, seeing in this intimate hour for the first time in years a vision of what each was and what they might be to one another.

The brothers were recognizing something fine and beautiful in Elsie, a culture far above their own, that told in every little word and glance. They were swelling with pride in her, and at the same time shrinking inwardly at their own short-comings. They rejoiced that she had not been too proud to come to them and cook for them, and they rejoiced most of all that she was beautiful and above them.

"Gee! This is great!" sighed Jack as he reached for his seventh doughnut. "Wouldn't it be simply ripping if you lived here all the time?"

"Not for Elsie," said Gene shortly with sudden gloom getting up and going over to the kitchen window, where he stood looking out with his back turned so that his sister could not see his face. His back, however, was eloquent. Elsie remembered it for many a night as she lay trying to think out her life and plan what to do.

At present, however, she only answered quietly: "I'm not so sure about that, Gene. I think it would be rather nice."

She hadn't intended saying it at all. She did not know until that moment that she had arrived in her thoughts even so far as that; but, having said it, she felt content to let it go, and was thrilled with the instant flash of joy in her brothers' eyes as they both wheeled and stared at her.

"My! Kid! You don't know how we'd like that!" said

Gene. "If you ever got where you could consider that, we'd do anything we knew how to show you a good time. This house has been an awful mess, you know, ever since mother died."

His voice died away wistfully.

"I know!" said Elsie softly, pitifully. "I'm afraid you thought me awfully selfish and hard-hearted; but, indeed, I never realized till the other day when I came out and found everything—well, you know—the way it was."

"Gee! Elsie if you come back and live, I'll stay in every evening, and play tiddleywinks with you!" declared Jack. "I'll get up and get your breakfast every morning, and dry the dishes nights, and you shall have half my pay!"

"Jack, why don't you buy a dear little single brass bed for your room? It wouldn't cost much," interrupted Elsie in the midst of a bear hug he was giving her.

"I will!" said Jack, bringing his fist down on the moulding-board till all the little uncooked doughnuts quivered. "Say, Elsie, will you go with me to buy it? Gee! Elsie but I certainly was glad to have those curtains. And you fixed my room up something fine. That dinky bed quilt and all the other little fillaloos! why, I like to wake up in the night now just to think where I am. It's pretty as a red wagon."

They rollicked through the afternoon, half playfully half seriously. Yet through it all Elsie knew that they had a great longing for her to be with them all the time, and she felt the drawing of their desire in her own heart. Two months before, if anyone had proposed her going home to live, she would have scouted the idea as impossible. She would have cried her eyes out at the thought of it, and have fled from the suggestion as if at the thought of a slavery. Now it seemed an altogether right and pleasant proposition, and she really felt a degree of pleasurable excitement in contemplating such a possibility. Besides, it was dear to have two big brothers wanting one. It was something so new and charming that Elsie forgot for the time being all that she would have to leave behind in going away from her aunt's.

It was growing dusk when the father came home, and Elsie had been thinking about staying to supper.

"I'll take you home, you know," said Jack wistfully. "And here comes Dad, too," he added, looking out of the window somewhat anxiously; then, after an instant's hesitation, during which he watched the coming figure intently, his voice rang out happily again, with something like relief in it, Elsie thought.

"Yes, that's Dad! He's all right, and he'll want to see you. Dad's been all kinds of curious to know who's been doing all this. He's come home straight, and early, too, to see if he can't catch you, I'll bet!"

Elsie with her cheeks prettily pink went forward to meet her father, and put up her lips to kiss him. There was no breath of liquor about him to-night. Jack had known that by some subtle sense when he had said, "Dad's all right."

She stayed to supper. Of course she stayed to supper. Could mortal girl resist the appeal she saw in all their faces?

Her father, after the first greeting, sank into a chair and watched her, alternately sighing and burying his face in his hands, his head bowed.

It was a beautiful supper, with Elsie in her mother's place opposite her father and the boys one on each side. They all felt as if it were a party, and the girl's cheeks blazed charmingly with all the pleasant compliments her brothers paid her, while the father sat and looked at her, and told her how she seemed as her mother did when he first met her.

After supper the boys helped wash up the dishes and then they all went to the piano. Elsie playing, the brothers standing around her, singing with her or listening, and watching her white fingers on the keys. Jack entirely forgot that he had a date with the fellows, and Gene shut his eyes to a game of poker he had promised to play that evening down at the clubrooms over the fire-house. When Elsie finally remembered that the people at home would be anxious about her, it was late indeed.

She had not realized how much this visit had meant to her father till she came to say good-by to him, and found his tears upon her cheek. He put his face down into her neck, and sobbed, and called her his little girl, and she suddenly knew that this sad, grave man loved her deeply. Why hadn't she known it before? Had it been right, even for her sake, to tear a family apart like that and separate their lives so thoroughly?

Jack took her home as he promised, and on the way she found out a good many things about her younger brother. For one thing she discovered that he had never finished the high school, had just quit because he and the teachers "didn't hit it," he said. He had gone to work where his mechanical skill and his natural brightness had brought him good wages, but he spent all without anything to show for it, and he was just drifting through life without any particular aim or ambition.

Jack was jolly and sociable. He could tell more jokes in a minute than anybody she ever met, and he was happy beyond expression to be seeing his beautiful sister home.

As they neared Aunt Esther's house, walking from the corner where they left the trolley-car, Elsie saw Bettina at the window looking out for her, and knew her escort would be recognized and that a storm was in process of preparation for her. She was glad that Jack laughingly declined to come in, and she bade him an affectionate good-by and went upstairs to the sitting-room to face what she knew was awaiting her.

BETTINA in the sitting-room window announced the arrival.

"Mother, there comes Elsie at last! And she has been to Morningside, just as I said. Jack's coming home with her. They're right under the electric light now. My! But Jack's grown awfully handsome! Really, Katharine, you ought to come here and look at him. He's really quite stunning."

"That's just what I was afraid of!" said Aunt Esther. "Elsie has been coaxed off there again; and she's slaving away her young life for that drunkard and his miserable sons, who are too lazy and shiftless to lift a finger to better their own condition. The next thing we hear her father will be saying that she has got to come home and live. And after we've had all the trouble of bringing her up and steering her through all the hard years of her life. I declare there's no such thing as gratitude in this world!"

"But, my dear!" said her husband, "she's their daughter and sister, you know. She owes them something. I think it's perfectly right she should go to see them often. In fact, I'm not altogether sure we're justified in keeping her here any longer. She's a woman, you know, and they are lonely men. Elsie could do a lot for her brothers if she wanted to. Suppose somebody should take Bettina and Katharine away from me."

"The idea!" said his wife. "As if anybody would dare! As if that was a parallel case! *You!* Don't for pity's sake compare yourself to George Hathaway. You! Why, of course you would take care of your children. But we have cared for Elsie as if she were our own, and now just when she has reached the age where we can enjoy her—"

"My dear, you didn't take Elsie so that you would be able to get personal enjoyment out of her some day, did you? I thought you took her to bring her up right."

"Of course, James! How you do quibble! But she has become like my own child, and I can't bear to have her spoiled now. Remember she's my dear sister's little girl."

"But, my dear, if your bringing-up of Elsie has been of any sort of use at all, she won't go back on it. She ought to be able to go on growing finer and better, and begin doing something in the world. I can't see that she could find anything much better or more natural than to make a pleasant home for her two brothers and her old father."

"Nonsense! She has her work in the world. The principal tells me she is going to be brilliant in several directions. He says she's doing a world of good among those dear girls of her class in high school. That's where she belongs. Not with old, hardened men who don't know in the least how to appreciate her."

"I'm not so sure her father and brothers couldn't appreciate her." This from the uncle. "George told me last winter that he was looking forward to the time when she would come back and make a real home in the old house again. He said it seemed as though life wasn't worth living without a woman there."

"The idea! As if he thought that lovely girl was going to spoil all her prospects in life going back to live with him! Why, he's nothing but a common working man, and he's fast getting to be a drunkard too. I don't see why you don't see that he has no business with her. I should think you'd see what it would do for her, just now when she's beginning to have a good deal of attention, and all. What kind of place would that be for her young men friends to visit her bye and bye and see that kind of a home and a father, and those wild brothers of hers? Any young man would stop and think twice before he went again after a girl to a place like that."

"My dear! If a young man cares no more for a girl than that, that he is scared away by her surroundings, I should say it would be a good try-out to see whether he is a real man or not."

"The very idea that that would be a test of manliness! I'm sure I think a young man would be entirely justified in leaving a girl if she didn't have proper relatives and a decent place to live. He would naturally think she wasn't of much account herself."

"Hush, Mamma!" warned Bettina, tiptoeing over to the sitting-room door. "Elsie has come in. I heard the front door shut some minutes ago. She will hear you."

An ominous silence succeeded, in the midst of which Elsie opened the sitting-room door. She had been slowly coming up the stairs, and had heard almost the whole conversation. Coming as she did fresh from the tenderer thoughts of her own family, it struck her like a sharp wind. She almost shivered when she heard her aunt's tone with regard to her brothers. Perhaps her aunt had reason to speak of her father in that tone for causes that she knew nothing about, but the brothers were children of her own sister as much as she herself was. Why should her aunt have that attitude toward them? Something true and keen rose up in her soul—was it her conscience?—and told her that Aunt Esther was wrong and Uncle James was right. For the first time, as she approached that sitting-room door, making no sound with her slow footsteps on the thick carpet, her own resolution crystallized, and she knew in her soul that she meant to go back to that other home, at least for a time, and see what she could do to make it happier for those who lived there. Having recognized her own position, she opened the door, and walked into the room.

It was not like Elsie to mince matters once she had decided; so now, though she saw the hostile attitudes of both aunt and cousins, she determined to speak out and have the matter over.

Katharine and Bettina, at the two front windows from which they had been watching for her coming, turned and looked at her. They knew her regal air, and understood that Elsie was about to throw down the gauntlet. Even in their annoyance with her they could but admire the grace and frankness with which she came straight to the point.

She walked over to her uncle, and stood beside him, feeling that he of them all would be most likely to understand her and take her part.

"Aunt Esther," she said gently, "I'm very sorry to be late to-night. I ought to have phoned you; but it got late before I realized it, and there wasn't any phone near by when I discovered the time. I supposed you would know where I have been, though, and would understand that I was all right."

"I'm sure I don't know why I would understand that if you have been out to Morningside. You certainly know I do not approve of your going there, and that it distresses me greatly to have you do as you have been doing the last three weeks."

"I'm sorry, Aunt Esther." Elsie drew a long sigh, and plunged in. "I'm very sorry. You and Uncle James have been just beautiful to me, and I don't like to think of distressing you; but sometimes there are things you just have to do, you know. I had to do this. I did indeed. And—I guess I better tell you the rest now. I'm afraid it will distress you still more, but you'll have to know it. Aunt Esther, I've got to go away from this beautiful home you've lent me the last five years. I've got to go back to my father's house. They need me there, and it's right that I should go. I've been thinking it over for three weeks now, and to-night I've decided. I hope you won't make it any harder for me than it already is."

She almost choked with a sudden sob that came into her throat as she thought of the pleasantness of all she was leaving, and she looked piteously now toward the aunt who had been like a mother to her since she lost her own. But her aunt's face was hard and bitter.

"It doesn't seem to have been so hard," she answered coldly, "when you can decide so easily."

"Oh, it hasn't been easy!" exclaimed the girl with a catch of her breath. "You don't know how hard it has been to think of leaving you all and going away from the things I love. But I couldn't get away from the thought of my father and my brothers living the way they are doing; and Auntie, if you could see the house as I have seen it, you would understand. You *couldn't* leave them that way. You know my mother wouldn't have wanted me to."

"It was all their own fault!" declared the relentless voice of the aunt. "Your father makes enough to have a comfortable home. There are plenty of servants and housekeepers that could be hired who would run the house and make things far more comfortable than you, an inexperienced young girl, could possibly do. Your father could have a good home if he chose to take the trouble to do so. If he doesn't choose, I don't see that you are called upon to give up your opportunities in life, and tie yourself down to living that way. You have your own life to live and yourself to think of. You can't do your school work justice if you take on the burdens of housekeeping. You surely are not going to give up and become a slave in your father's house."

"No, I am not going to give up school. I am going to have a good servant, and give her directions. I have got to go out there and make that place over, and have a cheerful home for my father and brothers."

The look her mother used to wear when she insisted on marrying the man they did not like came over the girl's face, reminding her aunt warningly of former years.

"Why, certainly, that is commendable, of course, if it doesn't take too much time from your other work. I'd be willing to secure a good servant for your father, and go out there occasionally and give her directions, say once a month, myself; and you might run out occasionally—motor out with some of your friends and drop in, just to show the maid there is somebody to watch her. But the idea of your going out there to live is ridiculous. It is impossible. I couldn't consent to it for a moment. That is no place for a young girl to be, in a house with three irresponsible grown men who wouldn't have an idea how to look after her comfort. It is what I took you away from, and I certainly do not intend that you shall return to it. Your uncle and I wish you to stay with us until such time as you see fit to go out and make your own home somewhere when the right time comes."

Elsie dropped into a chair, and took a deep breath; but

her firm little lips had not relaxed. She knew she must fight the battle to the finish, now that she had begun.

"Auntie, you do not understand," she said gently, speaking low. "It is not just a servant to keep the house in order they need. It is a woman in the house to love them and make things cheerful evenings when they come home. Have you ever stopped to think what there has been in Jack's life to make him want to grow up to be a good man? Did you ever realize what Eugene does with his evenings? Can you possibly know what it would be for my father to come home night after night to a dark, empty house, and have nobody there to be glad he had come? I've been there now for several Saturdays, and you can't think how desolate, how utterly dreary—"

"I can imagine how desolate and utterly dreary it will be for *you,*" interrupted her aunt pointedly.

"Well, why shouldn't I bear a part of it, if I can't make it better?" responded the girl quickly. "But I don't intend to bear it. I intend to make a change in it. I'm going to have the old piano tuned, and play a good deal, and sing with the boys; and I'm going to read to them sometimes; and we're going to make fudge, and have in some young people, and see if we can't make the old house cheerful again. Why, Auntie, it would have broken your heart if you could have seen my father's face when he found I was going to stay to supper to-night. I've *got* to go! I couldn't stand it not to go. It wouldn't be *right;* and, if you could just understand it all, you would say so too."

"Let her go!" said Katharine crossly. "Let her go try it, Mamma; it'll cure her quicker than anything else. Let her see what it is to stay at home evening after evening. No symphony concerts, no automobile rides, no invitations, no friends running in, no boxes of candy and American Beauty Roses! No Halsey Kennedy coming after her any more. He was sore as could be this morning because she wouldn't go motoring with us, and he hardly spoke all day. He'll go back to Celia Baxter if she doesn't look out. But let her go and try it. You'll see her back here again before the week's out, or I'll miss my guess."

Then Bettina.

"Elsie, I think you're just carried away with the idea of keeping house yourself and having two big brothers to see you around. But you'll find they won't pay you a bit of attention after you've been there a week. They likely have their girls and their friends and you've grown apart in all these years you've been separated. You can't possibly get together again just by going back there to live."

"Then we're going to grow together again," said Elsie with that firm little set of her lips like her mother. "Bettina, I thought after I got things settled you and Katharine and some of our friends in town here would come out often and help me."

There was a wistfulness in her tone which her cousins did not fail to notice and take advantage of.

"No, indeed!" tossed Katharine, flinging herself into a big chair indifferently. "You can't count on us. We're not foreign missionaries. I'm not going to give up my good times to go out to Morningside. If you can cut us out so easily, you'll have to get on without us. I might come out and call sometime, but I haven't time to spend bothering out there. You haven't any idea what you're doing, of course. You'll just have to go and try it, but anybody else could see with half an eye that you and your brothers are not going to hit it off together after you've been separated this way, you with an education and they with *none.*"

It was right then and there that Elsie, noting the curl

of her cousin's lip, resolved in her heart to change Katharine's opinion of her brothers or die in the attempt. Her eyes flashed and her lips quivered, but she held her ground firmly. She arose with a kind of sad finality in her manner, and gathered up her things.

"Well, you're all against me!" she said bravely with a tremble in her voice. "I had a feeling you would be, but I have to do it, anyway. He's my father, and they're my brothers, and they need me and want me; and I've *got* to go. I should *hate* myself if I didn't. And, besides, I really *want* to go."

Then her uncle spoke up. He had been watching her keenly all through the conversation. Now there was a light in his eyes as if he were pleased.

"No, we're not all against you, Elsie," he said. "I'm with you. I think you are doing just right. If you've got it in your heart to make a home for those who are your own flesh and blood, it would be criminal in us to stop you. It's your right and your privilege. And, much as we shall miss you, we ought to help you to do what you think is right. It's a beautiful thing you have chosen to do, and I'm proud of you for wanting to do it. Remember, though, that you have a second home here whenever you want it, and a place in all our hearts just the same as ever; and, if you ever get to a tight place where you need some one to help you or advise you, come to me, and I'll do my best. A girl that is willing to tackle a job like that is some girl, I tell you, and I'm proud to be uncle to her."

Then suddenly Elsie's courage gave way, and she went and flung her arms around her uncle's neck, and buried her face on his shoulder, while the tears took rapid possession of her. Her uncle patted her shoulder comfortingly, and it was all very still in the room. When Elsie finally got control of herself again, and lifted up her face apologetically, there was no one else there but her uncle and herself. They had all stolen out quietly. Elsie knew it was because they did not approve of her uncle's course toward her, and because they were unwilling to show her how sorry they were for her. They thought it would be better to let her suffer now, and so break down her purpose.

Her uncle patted her again and smiled.

"You're going to do a grand thing, child, and I'm sorry we can't all be unselfish enough to be glad for you. Your brothers need you, and you can do more than you realize. I guess your father needs you too. You'll do him good."

"I guess it will do me good, too, Uncle James," said Elsie meekly, trying to smile through her tears. "I've been living a pretty nice selfish life for the last five years. It's time I took some of the hardships."

"But you mustn't think we shan't miss you, child," said her uncle again with a sigh. "You've been like one of our own, you know, and we don't know the difference." Then he stooped and kissed her good-night. Elsie went up to her pretty room where the lamp was lighted, touching with a rosy glow the brass bed, with its blue satin eider-down comforter rolled at the foot, its pretty silver things on the little bird's-eye maple dressing-table, its blue and white draperies, its long mirror in the closet door that had been put in so she could see how her dresses hung, and all the pretty trifles that had been added to that room from time to time just to please her. She would have to leave it all and go to that other forlorn little room. Could she ever endure it? A sudden rush of tears again blurred the sight of the beloved things; and she shut the door quickly and locked it.

She could hear Bettina and Katharine talking in low, annoyed tones. She knew they were discussing her. She could hear her aunt walking about in her room on the other side of the hall, and she thought how it would be to be away from them every night; not to be at the pleasant supper-table, nor have the young people coming in the evening, nor go to the different entertainments together any more; and all at once it seemed more than she could bear, and she had an impulse to rush in and tell her aunt she had not meant it, that she could not go ever.

But instead she threw herself down on the pretty bed, and cried as if her heart would break.

After a little the enormity of her sacrifice dwindled somewhat, and she was able to look at things more sanely. She was able to remember once more the things that had called her out to Morningside, and made her really want to go and stay. She recalled her father's sad smile, and the wistful lighting of Jack's eyes when he had said how great it would be if she were there all the time. She thought of that row of photographs on Gene's bureau, and suddenly she felt sure once more that nothing could move her from her purpose. She would go and she would see whether there was not some way to make her brothers as interesting and attractive in the eyes of the world as if they too had been taken by Aunt Esther when they were younger and brought up as she had been. It should not be too late! She would see what she could do. She would make them go to college, perhaps. What if she should?

And in the sudden rush of thoughts over this idea she brightened up and prepared herself for retiring. But, when she lay down, it was not to sleep. Her mind went over and over the day's experiences: Her brothers' joy over finding her in the house; the bright things they had said and done; the way they had helped her and tried to make things easier; the gratitude they had so freely expressed. Her heart thrilled and thrilled again, and she knew perfectly now that no brass beds and silver-backed hair-brushes and satin coverlets, no, nor aunts, nor cousins, nor friends would be able to keep her from the course she had chosen to take. She had tasted the joy of service for love, and she could never be satisfied to live just for self again.

THE Sabbath was a rather unhappy day. Aunt Esther and the girls went about with gentle, hurt looks upon their faces, frequent sighs, and an abstracted, anguished air that wrung poor Elsie's heart. One or two attempts the girl made to win her aunt over to her way of thinking, but received only cold, bitter words concerning her father or else a rush of tears.

"Better let her alone a bit, little girl," whispered her uncle after Elsie's last attempt, when her aunt had left the room in tears. "She'll come to see and understand, and she knows in her heart it's right. That's what's hurting her. Just wait, and she'll come around and be proud of you all right, Elsie."

Elsie quite sadly said no more, but she did a good deal of thinking and planning.

Monday afternoon she took the trolley for Morningside. There were some things she must arrange before matters went any further, and now was the time to do it before Aunt Esther said anything more. She must have a talk with her father.

When she reached Morningside, she stopped at the

store, got some oysters, and ordered milk, crackers, celery, and a few other things sent up. It wouldn't take long to make an oyster stew, and she could talk while they were eating. She noticed some cut flowers in one of the shop windows, and went in and bought three big yellow chrysanthemums. Perhaps her father and brothers wouldn't care for them, but they seemed to brighten things up a lot for her and to give her courage to make the big changes that were before her.

It was half past four when she reached the house, and there was not much time to do a great deal. She went upstairs, and did a bit of tidying. A glance into her own room gave her a moment of homesickness. She would have to have that thoroughly cleaned before she could feel at home there. Would she ever feel at home? Well, never mind, so long as she made a home for the others!

She took the things out of the tiny closet, and carried them up to the storeroom. She dusted the bureau and the books and chairs, gave a hopeless look at the old walnut bedstead, and reflected that she must get together some bedding for herself if she were coming out to live. Then she shut the door, and went downstairs. It would be time enough to think about that room when she had to live in it. She wouldn't have to be in it much, anyway; so why worry? It would be only nights and mornings. There would be so much to be done she wouldn't have time to think of herself.

She went about dusting and putting things in order again. At half past five she put some potatoes into the oven to roast, set the table with the three big chrysanthemums in the middle in a tall glass pitcher, and got everything ready for supper. There were celery in a glass dish, a quivering mould of jelly, a plate of crisp crackers, and a dish of tiny little sweet pickles. The oyster stew was beginning to send a savory steam through the house when the bus arrived with the brothers.

Elsie ought to have seen their faces brighten when they caught sight of the flowers. What had happened? Not Elsie there again so soon! That would be too good to be true.

But, when they flung wide the kitchen door, and Jack gave a cheery whistle, there sure enough she was, running out of the kitchen to meet them, with her sleeves rolled high and a big apron enveloping her. The gaunt cat followed, amorously winding herself between Elsie's feet and actually purring hoarsely, an out-of-practice but quite genuine purr.

They just danced around her, those two big brothers, and whirled her off her feet with their joy. They shouted and whistled and sang and laughed until the neighbors across the way must have wondered what had come to the house of Hathaway.

The trolley stopped while they were in the midst of their rejoicing, and the father arrived, amazed at the noise. He came in as if not quite sure yet whether his senses were betraying him or not, and the daughter read a real welcome in his smile as he looked around with a kind of wistful contentment.

Elsie had telephoned her aunt that she was staying out to dinner that night, and would be home by nine o'clock if possible; so she had not a great while to remain, and must do her talking rapidly. After the oysters were brought in and everybody served she began:

"Father, I've been thinking of what you said about wanting me to come home. I think I'll come if I can manage it. You know I'm going to school in the city, and I'd have to be away all day—"

But the whoops of joy from her brothers interrupted her conversation for several minutes; and both big fellows left their seats, and came around to embrace her in their eagerness. When the uproar had somewhat subsided, she began again.

"I should have to have a good servant, father; do you think we could manage it? You know I shouldn't have much time to work. But I could teach her what to do, and I could be here evenings. I think we could have good times together."

The father lifted his whitening head and looked at her with yearning tenderness.

"You can have all the servants you want, child, if you'll just come back and put some soul into this old house," he said feelingly; and then he rested his forehead in his hands and groaned.

Elsie, deeply touched, came around to him and put her arms about his bowed head, kissing him tenderly, a strange new yearning coming into her heart. Why had she never realized before that she had left true and loving hearts for her own selfish ease? And yet they had been willing for her good to have her away all these years!

The father lifted his face after a time, and his cheeks were wet with tears.

"I'd like to have you come back, daughter, if you think it won't be sacrificing too much," he said in a shaken voice. "We maybe don't know how to make things look so fancy as they do at your aunt's house—we're only three lonely men, but we'll do the best we can to make you happy. I'm making enough to keep you well and get a servant too."

He patted her hand awkwardly. This beautiful grown-up daughter embarrassed him.

"It's been no home here since your mother left, but maybe you can bring home into it once more," he said tenderly.

Elsie and her brothers did the dishes before she left;

but they had to do some rushing, for Elsie did not wish to distress her aunt any more than necessary by being late. Both boys elected to escort her back to the city, and she bade her father good-by, promising to be out early Saturday morning to stay.

When the boys left their sister at their aunt's door, they walked on down the street in silence for several blocks. They were so absorbed in thought that somehow by common consent they had not thought to take the car.

"That's a big thing for her to do; do you know it, kid?" said Gene at last. "Did you get a look into that parlor window? That's some room compared to ours! See that fireplace with the fire shining on those brass andirons and the big lamp with the colored globe, and that big grand piano. She's leaving a lot to come out to our dump."

"Yes. And *some dump!"* breathed the younger brother contemptuously. "Say, why couldn't we have a fireplace? There's room enough on the side of the room where the mantelpiece is. I always did like to see an open fire."

"Tell Dad. Maybe he'll do something."

"I will!" declared Jack. "Gee! How'd we ever get to living in such a mess, anyway? I useta wish I would never see the dump again when I went away to school in the morning, and I useta wish I could die when I went home at night. Of course one doesn't mind when there's some place to go, but most times you want a spot to hang up in between."

"Same here," declared Gene. Then they walked several more blocks in silence.

Suddenly they found themselves in the business section and passing a large department store. Eugene came to a halt before a great window display.

The scene represented a room in a mansion, the walls hung with soft, neutral tints, the windows draped in white and rose, the cushions on the white willow chairs repeating the same tints. On the floor was a costly Oriental rug in which rose and gray and green predominated in lovely silkly blending. Before the little white dressing-table with its threefold mirror was seated a waxen lady in negligee robe of rose chiffon, with boudoir cap of rose and silver lace, toying with the silver-backed brushes and other articles of the toilet that lay upon the delicate lace-edged linen cover. Over at the other end of the room was a white chiffonier and a delicate bed with insets of wicker. The bed was covered with a costly spread of handsome openwork lace over pink satin, and at the foot was folded a puffy satin quilt of rose color.

"Some class!" ejaculated Jack, looking carefully at the details. "Say, Gene, we oughtta fix up her room. She fixed ours. What d' ya say? Let's do it."

"Take some cash to make up that outfit."

"Well, how much ya got? Guess I've got a hundred lying around, and Todd owes me fifty he borrowed last month. He promised to fork over soon."

"Guess I can match you once again," said Gene. "I've been saving up to buy a car when a good bargain comes along, but that can wait."

"We may want a car too, now," said Jack thoughtfully. "Wish I hadn't blowed in so much going up in aeroplanes and playing poker, but a fellow had to do something to pass the time away."

"Well, I guess we might manage to get some kind of an outfit together by Saturday if we make a good stab at it. What do you say to taking to-morrow off and seeing what we can do?"

The two went on reluctantly from that window to

others, gradually discovering what seemed to be the style in bedroom furnishings, noting the differences of qualities and shapes and colors, lingering long at a window filled with Oriental rugs.

At last they took the car for Morningside, still discussing which bedroom set had been the prettier, the one on Market Street or the gray one at Filleree's.

It was late when they reached home, and their father was asleep in his chair. They roused him, and poured into his ears their plans, taking him into the front room to show him where a fireplace might be built. They were so excited about it that they stayed up 'til midnight planning just where the chimney could go. They even took a candle, and all three went out-of-doors to see whether it would interfere with the windows upstairs if it were placed where they had planned.

When they went upstairs, Jack flung back his sister's door and turned on the light, going in with a critical look around. It was strange how Elsie's advent had changed the looks of everything. What had heretofore been the only tolerable tidy spot in the house, the shrine for a sort of ideal of womanhood, had now become a musty, dusty, gloomy spot, far too poor for the girl that was coming to occupy it.

"Gee! Isn't it fierce?" exclaimed Jack. "No wonder she never came back before! I s'pose she's used to fine things like those we saw in the windows to-night. Say, Gene, this wallpaper's rotten. It would give any girl the jimjams to wake up in a room like this. Couldn't we get it papered before Saturday if we put Harlin wise and made him hustle?"

"H'm! Maybe," said Gene, looking around. "It *is* fierce, isn't it? You couldn't put good things into a hole like this. S'pose you hustle over to Harlin's early in the morning before he sends his men out for the day. If you tell him that it's for a surprise, I guess he'll fix us up. Tell him we want something real snappy with roses in it."

Those two big boys could hardly sleep that night with their planning. They were almost as excited as if they had been girls, and Jack was up and off bright and early in the morning.

Harlin was an old friend. He remembered Elsie when she was but three, with eyes like stars and hair of gold. Surely he would help them get the room ready for her by Saturday. He was rushed, of course, and behind in his work; but what was one day or so, more or less? He would put somebody else off. Small room, was it? Well, he had the very thing, left over from the Graham mansion on the pike.

It might not sound so very grand just to tell about it, but it made up "simply great!" "Gray felt, real light, with a ceiling of rose tint and a border of cut-out roses on the gray, and you wouldn't believe how pretty it finished off," said the man. "I went up to see it when it was furnished, an' it was just like a parlor. They had two kinds o' curtains, one white with a border of pink roses, and one pink; an' the room all looked as if the sun just shone right in. It went real pretty with the gray wall. You wouldn't a' b'lieved it, but it did."

Jack wasn't quite sure; but the roses sounded good, so he told Harlin to go ahead, and Harlin promised to send someone over that morning to begin.

Jack rushed home, and moved all the furniture out of the room, bundling it unceremoniously up into the back room.

"It'll do for the servant, won't it?" he asked, practically. "Anyhow, we have to have a decent place for her to sleep, or we couldn't get one to stay. That Rebecca wasn't worth her salt."

"I should say!" answered Gene. "Now come on and hustle. We've got a lot to do to-day."

The brothers rushed off to their unwonted shopping as eager as two children.

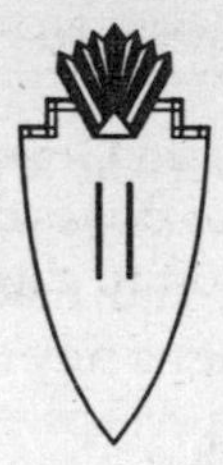

ALONG toward six o'clock the brothers returned, weary but well satisfied with their labors. They had purchased carefully and with due deliberation and many appeals to sympathetic salesmen and saleswomen, and they felt that they had purchased well. A little white bed and bureau and desk; a white willow rocker with rosy cushions; a small white desk-chair; filmy curtains with a border of roses; a lace-edged cover for the bureau; and a lace-edged, rose-bordered, fat pin-cushion; a silver-backed brush and comb; a pink-bordered blanket and coverings for the bed; an eider-down quilt of pink satin like the one they had seen in the window display; and, crowning extravagance of all, a small but very Oriental rug, just large enough to fill the space between the bed and the bureau, and extend from near the door to near the window, where the little rocker would sit. The rug was a bargain and very silky, with a lot of deep rose color and cream in its design; and the brothers, as they settled down into their seats in the trolley-car, drew a long breath of satisfaction over it. They knew that Elsie would probably know the value of that rug, and they fairly beamed with delight over the thought that they had been able to buy it for her. Only in a vague way did they appreciate it themselves, and that from hearsay rather than knowledge. It was just a tiny rug. It looked to them no better—not so good, perhaps—as a larger rug for the same price that would have covered the entire floor and was gay with roses and lilies; but they had been most thoroughly instructed in rug lore by the various salesmen who had waited upon them that morning, and they had learned that this small, glowing fabric was related to a great rug that hung high upon the wall that counted its hand-made knots to the square inch by the hundreds and its price by the thousands of dollars; therefore they sat in awe, and reflected upon their purchase with deep satisfaction.

When they reached home, they did not stop to start their supper nor even to light up. They made one dash up the stairs to the little room that was their sister's. Yes, Harlin had been as good as his word. There was a smell of new paste in the air, and the floor was littered with old paper torn and scraped from the walls. They stumbled in it as they reached to turn on the light.

The work was not all done, but it was well on its way. The ceiling glowed down rosily upon them, and two walls were smooth and gray with a ravishing rose vine clambering neatly over the top and blending ceiling and side wall. They could see that it would not take long to finish. It would probably be done when they got home to-morrow night from work.

"Say! It's all right!" commented Jack delightedly.

"It's not so bad," rejoiced Eugene. "Our curtains 'll go well with that border. But this paint is fierce. It ought to be white; what was that they called the furniture? Ivory-white? It ought to be painted ivory-white. Guess we better get a pot of paint, and get at it to-morrow night. It won't take long."

"The floor too. We'll have to get up that matting, and stop up the cracks with putty, and paint it, and varnish it, I guess. What color? I guess mahogany would set off that rug pretty well. What's the matter with getting the paint to-night? Then we can go right at it when we get home to-morrow. Guess it won't do to knock off another day. We might need the money with all these things to pay for."

"Somebody ought to be here when the things come to-morrow."

"I guess we can get Harlin to look after those."

While they were making their plans, the father arrived, and came straight upstairs as eager as either of them. It was eight o'clock before they got around to sit down to their supper, and it was a very different atmosphere from that of their usual meals, for all of them were talking animatedly and suggesting things that might be done to make the house more habitable and pleasant for the new occupant.

"There's plenty of room to build a sleeping-porch out that south window of hers," suggested the father eagerly. "Most of the houses out here have one or two of them. That would be something she doesn't have in the city, anyway."

"Just the thing, Dad. Isn't it a pity we didn't think of these things last summer, and get them done when we had plenty of time?"

"It's better this way," said the father. "We shouldn't know how she wanted everything, you know. She'll have her own ways, and it's best to let her plan it herself."

The brothers looked at one another with sinkings of heart. For the first time it occurred to them that their purchases might not be all that their sister would have liked, and perhaps they ought to have waited until she came.

"Well, everything can be exchanged if she doesn't like it," reflected Jack cheerfully, and so a degree of satisfaction was regained.

Tuesday night the papering was done, and the boys began their painting. The air was so full of excitement that they hardly stopped to eat. The father hovered between the room upstairs, giving advice to the boys, and downstairs, where the new furniture was assembled in parlor and hall. He touched with reverent finger the fine white finish, looking wistfully into the French plate mirror that reflected the tired old image of what he used to be. He wondered vaguely whether his wife could know that their little girl was coming back to the old home to live, and whether she was glad. He felt a pang of fear lest Elsie might not like it enough to stay, lest, after all, her aunt might yet persuade her not to come. Indeed, this thought was just below the surface in the minds of them all, and they worked the more nervously that they might not think it out to their consciousness.

Jack got up at four o'clock Thursday morning to put the last coat of paint on so that it would be dry enough by night to hang the curtains. They were so impatient to see the whole finished room that they could hardly sleep. Thursday evening they ate crackers and cheese with coffee, taking as little time as possible, that they might get to work at once.

They washed their hands very carefully when they began to handle the white furniture, and set every piece in place as if it were an ark of the covenant and they were unfit to touch it. They took off their heavy shoes, and went about in stocking feet, lest they scratch the floor; and every time they put anything in place they stepped back with bated breath and surveyed the result, as bit by bit the lovely room was built.

As a lady might have put the last exquisite finishes of lace and jewelry to her costume, so they fastened up the little brass rods, and hung the cheap muslin curtains with rose-bordered ruffles; so they laid on the lace-edged bureau-cover, and set forth the fat pink-satin cushion.

With careful hands and much adjuring of one another they spread up the bed, even to the final arranging with clumsy fingers of the big pink eider-down quilt across the foot. Three or four times apiece they unfolded and replaced that eider-down before they could get it to suit them both, and there was much disputing as to how those they had seen in the shop-windows had been folded. But at last it was all done, and the lovely rug spread down in the centre space; and then the three men stood just outside the door, and took in the whole finished beauty, as if it were a sanctuary, without saying a word.

The beauty of it lingered with them when they slept; they dreamed, and thought they were looking into the kingdom of heaven, where the roses grew high against celestial skies and the streets were inlaid with jewels like an Oriental rug.

Neither of the brothers came home in the bus Friday evening. Each, unknown to the other, got off from work early, and slipped away on an errand before coming home. Eugene started first and went to the city. When he came home, it was still afternoon, and no one was about. He stole up to the house shamefacedly, and up to the new room. There he stood a moment looking about, filled with that wonder that ever impresses one at a miracle of change. Then with a flush of embarrassment upon his face he opened his parcels, disclosing a long, soft, rosy robe of thin silk and lace, and a lovely little silver-lace boudoir-cap wreathed with satin rosebuds. It had taken courage and perseverance to purchase those articles, and now he felt foolish standing there and holding them. Would what Jack think of him? What would Elsie? Yet somehow his soul had not been satisfied until he went and bought them, silly, useless baubles though they were. He had wanted them there to give that touch of woman's personality to the room, that little bit of feminine beauty that would show their sister the room was hers, even before she had stamped it with her own possessions.

He arranged them clumsily at last across the back of the desk-chair with an attempt at imitation of the way they had lain across the chair in the store-window. Then he stepped back in the shadow of the hall, and looked again.

While he stood thus, and before he was aware, Jack came stealing in with his arms full of bundles, and started back with an embarrassed laugh at seeing his brother. In fact, it would have been hard to tell which brother felt the more sheepish at being caught in what he was doing. Jack recovered first, and came springing up the last three steps at a bound, and stood looking into the room. Then he tiptoed across, and looked at the cap and gown approvingly.

"Good work, old boy!" he applauded joyously. "I didn't know you had it in you. I don't know what they're for, but they seem to belong. Now just cast an eye at what I've got."

He sat the largest package on the floor, and went into the bathroom with the others. In a moment he returned carrying two slender crystal vases, one holding a single perfect rose, white with a flush of rose color in its heart. This he set upon the top of the little white desk. The other vase held half a dozen glorious pink buds, and this he set on the bureau, where the flowers were reflected in the mirror and sent their fragrance through the room.

"Some class, Jack! You've beat me to it!" declared his elder brother.

"Not yet," said Jack, and rushed out for his other package. This was two pictures, delicate pastels framed in silver, one a bit of ocean, real and vivid, green waves flecked with white foam, the other a bit of brook and birch-tree, with the evening sky all rose and silver in the west behind the etching of fine branches.

He hung the pictures in the two bare places on the wall that had seemed to cry out for something, and then they stood back to take in the effect.

Outside, the trolley-car was stopping. Something moved Jack to step to the window and look out.

"She's come. Elsie's come! Let's beat it downstairs!"

And, gathering up the papers and the hammer, they made a hasty retreat to the kitchen, from which they presently issued decorously as if they had not thought of being anywhere else.

BREAKFAST at Aunt Esther's that Friday morning had been a very sad and dreadful affair. Aunt Esther's eyes had that wan look, a bit red around the edges that said she had been crying half the night. It was not unbecoming for Aunt Esther to cry, but it was depressing. Elsie was made to feel that she was the cause of the deep grief. She felt almost desperate; yet, as the days of that last week had dragged themselves by, she had been more and more convinced that her duty lay at Morningside, and not in this home where everything was so perfect and lovely.

The two cousins were absorbed in their mail, which had lain by their plates as they entered. All the week they had treated Elsie with a gentle, condescending patience that one accords to very young naughty children, who are not only giving us pain, but are hurting some one very dear to us. They were doing their best to show Elsie she was an ungrateful girl to reward their dear mother for all she had done for her, by running away.

Uncle James had exploded a bomb in the midst of this scene by suddenly laying down his paper and saying to his wife:

"My dear, if Elsie still thinks that her place is at Morningside, and she is intending to go there tomorrow, I think we should see about sending her things out today for her. She will want her own furniture and everything that is in her bedroom, of course."

There was dead silence, during which Elsie gasped and tried to get voice to answer; but she could only cast one grateful glance at her uncle and then struggle with the tears that threatened to get the better of her. Her two cousins looked up with a glance of disapproval that said as plainly as words could have done that their father was simply crazy to mention such an idea; and Aunt Esther put on a severe front, and finally spoke.

"No, James, I don't intend to send Elsie's things out to Morningside at present. It would be a useless expenditure of time and money. Elsie will soon discover that her wild, quixotic attempt is impossible; and then she will have to come back, and the things would have all the wear and tear of the moving. Let Elsie first put her fine theories to the test and see if she can endure Morningside before we attempt to sugar-coat Morningside for her further blinding. Elsie had better see her father's home as it is—as it was when we took her from it—and then she will be able to judge which she prefers for her home."

It was a cruel speech, and stabbed Elsie to the quick. She cast one anguished glance at her aunt, and rose from her place at the table, looking toward her uncle.

"Uncle James," she said, and her voice was trembling with sobs that she was holding back, "you are very kind; but Aunt Esther is right. It is better for me to go to my father's house as it is, and not take any of the luxuries of this life that you have so kindly spread around me. I thank you for the thought, but I couldn't possibly take anything away from the lovely room I have occupied. I would rather think of its being here just as I left it. Besides, I am my father's daughter and I should be content with such things as he can furnish me. Please don't worry about it; I shall be all right. And please excuse me now; I shall have to hurry to catch my car."

With this speech and a great choke in her voice Elsie managed to leave the room without utterly breaking down.

She went quickly up to her room, cast a few last things into her trunk that stood packed and ready, locked it, put the key into her pocket, and hurried downstairs. The good-bys were very hard. Aunt and cousins kissed her coldly and turned away in hurt silence. Elsie tried to speak but broke down in sobs. But her uncle put a comforting arm about her and said, "Never mind, little girl. Things won't always seem dark. I honor you for what you are doing, but remember we love you, and this home is yours whenever you need it."

She stopped at an express office, and left an order for a man to call and take her trunk to Morningside.

She wrote a brief little note to her aunt, saying that she thought it best, under the circumstances, that she should not return that night to cause them any more pain, and she hoped they would forgive and love her again sometime. This note she sent by a messenger boy. Then she went to the stores, and bought a few things she knew she would need in her new life, and would have no other opportunity to buy. These included some simple inexpensive bedding for her own room; and she was much troubled when she found it could not be sent out until the next morning. However, she decided to make the best of it. She could surely get along for one night, especially if her trunk reached there before night.

Her purchases had delayed her, so that it was almost

supper-time when she reached Morningside and entered dubiously the house she meant to try to make a home.

With a sigh she threw down the packages she was carrying, and began to take off her hat and coat. A sense of defeat seized her. She wondered whether, after all she had not been, as her aunt said, "quixotic" in her action. Perhaps it was true that life out here would be intolerable to her. Perhaps she would see it when it was too late to retreat and after she had hurt the dear ones who had been real father and mother and sisters to her. And there was that dusty little dark room upstairs. She must go up and face it now. There was no putting it off till another time. She must sleep there to-night. She had, as it were, burned her bridges behind her, and could not return. Disagreeable as it might be, that ugly, empty room upstairs was her one retreat from an uncongenial world. What had she been thinking about to dare to make this final move?

In the dim light of the hall spectres of her little childhood came out and grimaced at her. Sad times when her mother was sick, and poor servants ruled the house. Times when her father had been inadequate to the situation, and her brothers had been noisy and unfeeling. All the lovely five years that intervened between that time and this receded, and allured her, and made her heart cry out after it as she was giving it up. This was her final surrender, this her moment of sacrifice. But the only audible evidence of it was that sigh.

The two big, eager boys in hiding in the pantry heard that sigh with alarm. They looked at each other as if a momentous thing had happened. The sigh seemed to menace all their hopes, and strike at everything they had tried to do; and their faces went blank with a startled fear. Then a sudden revelation came to them of what it must be to leave a home such as their sister had left, and come to this dull, lonely place with shadows and dust to welcome her. Simultaneously they broke forth from their hiding boisterously, with perhaps the same idea, of comforting her and tiding her through this, her first hard moment of real homecoming.

The sighs were forgotten in the boys' rough and joyous greeting. They seemed to outdo their own shy, naturally reserved natures, and to have polished their wits for the occasion. Their spirits effervesced and bubbled over with fun and wit, and Elsie's sighs turned into laughter.

Jack turned on the lights all over the first floor as if to celebrate, and, seizing his sister, whirled her around and around, finally landing her in the big chair in the front room. Gene hurried to get her a glass of water, and all the time they were noisily telling her how glad they were that she had come to-night instead of waiting until to-morrow. It never occurred to any of them that there was such a thing as dinner, and nothing in the house to get it with, or, at least, very near to nothing. They just sat together, and talked nothings, merely happy to be there together and know that they belonged, that this pleasant thing they had been hoping for had come to pass, and they were of the same household at last. At last, this was what the boys felt. And Elsie forgot her fears and her pangs of conscience, and knew for a surety that she had been right in coming.

The pleasant dinner-table at her aunt's, with all its attendant comforts and delicious odors and tastes and beauties, faded from her vision. The dust and forlornness of this place faded also, and she was just in the dear place where she was loved and belonged. She forgot that there was a dreary little room upstairs where she would have to go by and by and make it into an abiding-place for herself. She was genuinely glad she was here, drawbacks, dust, dismalness, and all.

And now that she was here, and the room upstairs ready to the last little perfection they knew how to procure, those two big, foolish men-children took a panic lest she should go up and see it. It suddenly seemed to them to have been an audacious thing for them to do. They ought to have waited and let her choose her own wall-paper and furniture. They ought to have given her perhaps some other room, a bigger, brighter one. They ought not to have gone into the little details so thoroughly, presuming to pick out a lady's decorations and even her adornments. Their faces burned with consciousness, as if that room could flare itself right down through the ceiling, and flaunt its rosy colors in their faces, and declare that they had done it. And so they worked with all their might to keep her from going upstairs.

Not that she was anxious. She was having a good time there. She would put off the dreary little room till it was time to sleep. Why worry about it? She could go to sleep at once when she got in it, and forget it.

Presently the father came, wondering at the sounds of hilarity and the bright lights; and then all at once Elsie realized that the primary duty of a woman in a home is to see that her family is well fed; and there had not been a thing done to get this one fed at all!

Pell-mell they all rushed to the kitchen to take account of stock. A few potatoes in the basket, enough to roast. Elsie ordered them washed and put in the oven at once. Not a scrap of meat in the house, and only two eggs! It was after six o'clock, and the store was closed. No chance to replenish the larder.

"Well, I'll make some waffles!" she declared, rummaging in the closet to make sure the waffle-iron was there. So, while Gene scrubbed away at the black old waffle-iron, and her father and Jack followed her orders, putting on butter, milk, jelly, and molasses in lieu of maple-syrup, Elsie stirred up her waffle batter.

That was a great supper, as they sat around the kitchen table to be handy to the waffle-iron so that nobody need be away baking. Nothing else could have made them so forget that they were new together as that impromptu kitchen supper.

And when it was over, and everything was in order, they lingered still, about the piano, singing. And all the while the thought of that little room upstairs was growing more and more insistent in all their minds, till finally the old father could stand it no longer, and suggested that Elsie would be tired and they had better be sending her to see whether she could make herself comfortable in any of their rooms for the night.

So at last Elsie herself made a move, and, catching up her hat and bag, declared she must go up and make her bed. All at once she remembered that her trunk had not come yet, and wondered what could be the meaning of it, and how she was to get on without it. Had Aunt Esther refused to let it go, or had the expressman forgotten? If it was due to Aunt Esther, Elsie felt she would never ask for her trunk. The sense of hurt from those she loved stung her as she went upstairs, and made her conscious once more of the strange place and new surroundings. Her feet lagged as they neared her door, and her hand sought idly for the place to turn on the light. She wanted nothing else so much as to cry.

Then the light sprang on, and she stood transfixed. What fairy-land was this to which she had entered? What exquisite bower for a lady fair? She passed her hand over her eyes and rubbed them. She could not believe her senses. She turned, and looked back down the stairs she had just mounted, to make sure she was in her right mind and this was really her father's house. Then she looked again.

Yes, it was all true. The ugly bed of clumsy fashion had vanished. The seedy rug was no more. The dusty bureau and rickety bookcase were gone. And in their place were fair, beautiful furnishings fit for a princess.

She looked on the white bed made with such clumsy precision, touched the rosy stain eider-down quilt, noted the soft gray walls ending in roses, the curtains, the bureau, the desk with its rosy-shaped lamp, the roses, and the little, foolish negligee; and tears of happiness stood in her eyes. Then all at once she knew that they stood for love, a great, new, glad love that had come to welcome her in her new home; and her heart overflowed in a cry of surprised joy.

It never even once occurred to her to wonder whether perhaps her aunt and uncle might have done this. She knew they had not. They would never have made it so attractive to her away from them. She knew the dear people downstairs, who were keeping so wonderfully quiet down there, had done it, to let her know how glad they were she had come.

With that one little cry of joy she dropped the things she was carrying, and sprang forward into the room. She seized the little rose silk gown, and threw it on about her shoulders. She pulled the silly little fretwork of silver and rosebuds down about her pretty hair; and, taking one of the rosebuds from the vase on the bureau, she fastened it at her throat. Then she turned and flew softly down the stairs with a quick little pleased sound and with a great light in her eyes.

The three big men who stood there with bated breath watching for her coming, fearful of her coming, hoping and dreading in their childishness what she might say or think, broad, helpless, self-conscious smiles on their faces, were overwhelmed with the beauty of her in her fantastic garb, with the little crown of silver stuff on her head and the rose at her throat.

The two brothers fairly beamed under her delight, and the jealous father hastened to say that he would have a sleeping-porch built out of her room if she would like it, and they were going to have a fireplace made in the parlor. The man was coming Saturday afternoon to make estimates.

And then they all had to go up to the beautiful new room together, and look at everything, and talk it all over again. And in the midst of it the expressman arrived with Elsie's trunk, although it was after eleven o'clock. He had got lost, and had been wandering around Morningside for two hours.

There was just room for the trunk between the desk and the foot of the bed, and the boys unstrapped it with many flourishes. It was so good to have her come to stay! Something really happening in the old house after all these years of famine! It was *great!*

The heart of the old house seemed to be throbbing joyously when at last everything was quiet and they all lay down to sleep. Elsie in her lovely rose-lined nest lay down most happily, her face wreathed in smiles, her eyes alight. She had not a thought of being lonely. Not even a thought of the lovely bed and the blue satin eider-down quilt she had left behind. For wasn't rose-color as lovely as blue any day? This couldn't be called a sacrifice with somebody ready everywhere to make things beautiful for her. Whatever the future days might hold in store for her, this night had been perfect. She drew a deep breath, and snuggled down beneath her soft coverings, conscious of the breath of roses, of the shimmer of the moonlight as it glanced across the silver picture-frames and glinted on the frostwork of the silver cap. How glad they were, those two boys! How dear they were! How wonderful of them to go to all that trouble to get that room ready for her! How they had outdone anything she had tried to do for them! It was just too great for words! The cap—and the gown—and the roses!

So she drifted off to sleep, thinking of the light in their eyes when she came downstairs in her butterfly garments.

IN THE gray dawn of Saturday morning Elsie stole downstairs softly. Her brothers and father had to leave for their work at half past six. They had adjured her not to wake up so early; they were quite used to getting a bite for themselves, but Elsie had no intention of letting them do so. She meant to begin right. Of course when the maid came she would prepare breakfast for them all, but this was Saturday morning with no school; so the girl enjoyed the thought of having breakfast ready.

To be sure, there was not much material in the house to work with for a substantial breakfast for three men, but one could always do something. It would be fun to surprise them. There was no chance to get anything at the store so early; so she must do what she could.

The milk had come, and she took the bottles in with satisfaction. She could make some milk toast, for there had been more than half a loaf of bread left the night before. Then she could fry the potatoes that were left, and make coffee.

A careful search of the rather bare cupboard discovered a small end of a ham, and this she seized upon gratefully. Then she remembered that up in her bag were two big oranges. These she could cut in halves, and set around at the places; and really her menu was not so bad, after all.

She carefully arranged the table, with the orange halves at each plate before she began her cooking; and then she closed the kitchen and pantry doors to keep the smell of ham and coffee from going upstairs and spoiling her surprise; but long before the three men were ready to come down, the coffee and toasting bread and frying ham had stolen through the cracks and crannies and penetrated with their festive odors.

"Gee! She's downstairs getting breakfast!" murmured Jack as he searched for his collar-button. "Say! That's great!" and he hustled down to help.

But Elsie had it all on the table ready for them, curtains drawn back, and the room bright with the morning sunlight.

"It looks most too good to leave," said her father, sitting down at the table and looking around. "Seems as if we ought to stay and enjoy it lest it might be gone."

"It will not be gone, Father. I intend to make it better than this as fast as I can. Now, what directions have you for me? I'm going to hire a servant this morning, and get her started in the routine of the house so she can carry things on later when school begins. Have you any choice which of the grocery-stores I patronize, and can I have things charged?"

There was pleasant, eager converse about ways and means during the meal, and, when the bus came and the car was heard in the distance, Elsie bade them all good-by quite cheerfully, and hurried up to her room for her hat. She meant to have that servant before she did another thing, if it were a possible thing to get her.

A pretty girl with determination can do a good many

things, and before another hour was up Elsie had found an oldish colored woman who was willing to come at once.

Elsie went back to the house immediately, stopping only to give an order at the store. In another hour the new maid presented herself and the business of rejuvenating the old house began.

When dinner-time came and with it the three men of her household, Elsie found herself really weary, but very eager and glad to see them.

The general sense of comfort and cleanliness that pervaded the place had its very visible effect on father and brothers. It seemed to stimulate them to be more careful about themselves. The boys refused to eat till they had made elaborate toilets; and, when Elsie saw how nice they looked when they came down, she was glad she had taken time to change from her work-dress into a bright little house-dress.

After supper the man came about the fireplace, and after he left Elsie began to order the furniture changed all around.

"Everything must be set with the fireplace as the centre now, you know," she declared, and in no time the brothers whirled the piano into the place she selected for it. It almost seemed that since she had spoken the fireplace was really there in shadowy form, with a phantom fire all laid ready for lighting.

"This room needs papering," said the father, walking about and looking at the walls critically. "It hasn't been papered for seven years or more, I guess. You go over and see what Harlin's got, Elsie, and have him do this room up as soon as the fireplace is finished."

"Father, dear, I'm afraid I'm putting you to an awful lot of expense!" cried Elsie in mingled delight and apology.

"It's time the old house was fixed up," said the father. "Now you're here there's some reason for doing it. The boys and I didn't seem to care what became of us. We didn't stay around except to sleep. But now it's different. I can stand the expense, I guess. There's a little money in the bank I haven't touched yet—your mother saved. I guess she'd like some of it used this way. She said it was for schooling, but somehow there wasn't any call for that. The boys didn't seem to care for any more education, and you were looked out for. Besides, I'm making a good salary, and it ought to go farther than I've made it. It's just sifted through my fingers somehow."

The boys looked at each other significantly; and Elsie caught the glance, and thought she knew what it meant. It was good, perhaps, to give her father legitimate expenses that he had to meet so that he would not spend his money in drink. This drink question was such a dark, mysterious unknown force for her to fight against. She must go slowly and carefully, and try to understand.

"Well, that will be delightful," she said happily. "There are a few things we need to get. This room ought to have a new rug, and this one should go into the dining-room. That carpet is all worn out. Some one will trip in that hole by the door, I am afraid. There are a couple of chairs that ought to be re-covered, too. I think we could manage that ourselves if we got the stuff. I don't want to spend much of that money mother saved, because really it ought to go for the object she saved it for, you know. The boys aren't either of them very ancient yet, and they ought to go to college."

She exploded this bomb in the room very quietly, as if she had said, "It is time to go to bed," and the two young men suddenly sat down in the two chairs that were nearest to them, and looked at her in astonishment. Then Jack gave a great shout of derision.

"College!" he yelled. "Some chance! Gene's twenty-three. He'd make a fine show in college, wouldn't he? As for me, I'd be an old man before I got ready to enter! Gee! That's a good one! Us in college!"

"Why not?" asked Elsie quietly. "Men have gone to college even older than twenty-three. Better late than never. How far did you go in high school, Gene?"

"Graduated," growled Eugene darkly, kicking his toes angrily against the table-leg. He was angry with himself for having been fool enough not to get an education when he might. He surmised that his sister was discovering that they were not her equals intellectually.

"How about you, Jack?" went on the calm voice of the sister.

"Quituated!" answered Jack sullenly.

"When?" asked Elsie quickly. "How much more of high school had you still?"

"Two years!"

"You could make that up this winter, and be ready to enter college next fall. I could help you get ready for your examinations."

"No chance!" said Jack dryly and decidedly.

"Why not? Wouldn't you like to go to college?"

"Sure! Like it well enough." Jack's tone was most indifferent. "But I couldn't ever get back to study. I never did study, anyhow, I just fooled. And it's too late now. I couldn't ever take examinations."

"Of course you could," said Elsie decidedly. "We'll get at it next week and look up how far you've gone. You ought to begin at once to get ready. You'll need English and mathematics and Latin. I'm not just sure what else, but I'll find out Monday. A friend of mine has a brother who just entered the university by examination, and she knows all about the requirements."

Jack looked at her with a sort of stunned admiration.

He wasn't going to take those examinations, of course! No sir! Not study, either! Not much! But it was nice to have a sister who cared.

"You're like your mother, Elsie," said her father with one of his deep sighs that was almost a groan; "she never would give up an idea once she got it started, and she was very ambitious. If she'd lived, I expect they both would have gone to college. Gene would have been through by this time."

Then Elsie spoke.

"Gene, why can't you enter the university this fall? You could, you know, if you have your credits from the high school."

Gene sat back and stared at her in astonishment.

"Me go to the university," he echoed stupidly. *"Fat chance!"*

"Why not?" asked Elsie insistently. "Thc tuition isn't much, and you could board at home. Father said there was money laid up for it. You ought to get your education at once. It isn't right for you to settle down to being just a laboring man. You have brains, and ought to be using them. Besides, if you are to be a laboring man even, you ought to be the best kind of one you can; and an education will make you better able to rise in whatever you are going to do in life."

They talked long that night, Elsie eagerly, persuasively, both boys as stubbornly set against her suggestions as could be, yet looking in the face for the first time in their lives, earnestly and squarely, the question of an education. They began to see it was possible, as their sister said; but it looked like a task to which neither felt himself equal. If studying had been something heavy to lift, or a hard battle to fight, or a race to be run, either of them would have undertaken it for her sake; but education was an unknown land into which they hesitated to enter, feeling themselves unqualified to star among its inhabitants. Therefore they stubbornly adhered to that one answer to all her eagerness. "No chance!"

Nevertheless, when Elsie finally went up to her little rose chamber, she had a memory of deep looks of thoughtfulness in the eyes of both of her brothers; and she had by no means given up the effort. The last thought she had left with them as she mounted the stairs to her room had been the suggestion that her brothers would make splendid athletes, and as for herself she would be proud to have them on the varsity football team or playing basket-ball. She could see that the suggestion interested both of them, for each began to tell of his experiences in playing and what he might have done if he had had the chance.

Perhaps it was a low motive to hold out for an inducement to an education; but, if it proved to be a lure, merely because it gave some common ground on which they could put themselves in a good light in the eyes of the university, it might lead to higher, better things.

When Elsie knelt beside her bed that night, she prayed earnestly for her two brothers, and that they might be led to want to make the best of themselves.

IT WAS at the Sunday morning breakfast-table that Elsie exploded her second bomb in the form of a simple question, "What time do you go to church?"

Now, the men of the Hathaway household had not been accustomed to rise on Sabbath mornings before eleven or twelve o'clock; and it had been their habit to sit around in their shirt-sleeves, collarless, unshaven, until such times as they individually saw fit to fix up and saunter out in search of something interesting to pass away the time. To go to church had not been even remotely within their scheme of life. The boys had stopped attending Sunday school when their mother died, and they had all drifted away from any connection with any church whatever. It had not occurred to them until this minute that Elsie's coming would need to make any difference in their Sabbaths except to make them more cheerful.

True, they were seated about the breakfast-table arrayed in clean shirts and collars, with shaven faces and hair immaculate, and that at the unearthly hour of nine o'clock on this Sabbath morning; but there had been noises of stirring in the kitchen for nearly two hours, and savory odors stealing upstairs to lure them down; and there sat Elsie at the foot of the table, pouring coffee, adorable in the little pink silk negligee and silver, rose-trimmed cap. How could mortal man resist coming down early on Sunday morning under circumstances like that? But church! Now, that was asking too much.

Jack laid down his knife and fork, and turned his attention for the moment from his hot muffin to burst out in a loud guffaw of amusement; but, his eyes met those of his brother, and the laugh was squelched in the beginning. Silenced he sat staring thoughtfully at Gene, the fun gradually fading from his eyes and instead came a look of surprise and a dawning understanding.

Gene had given him the "high sign." Church! Of course Elsie had been accustomed to going to church; and, if she was to be happy at Morningside, she must miss nothing she enjoyed from the old life, if they could possibly help it. Of course she must go to church if she really wanted to—it was inconceivable that she could; but, if she did, why, perhaps some one would have to go with her. Gene was the proper one, of course; he was the older; though it wouldn't be so bad to walk beside such a trim, pretty girl as Elsie and let the highbrows at church see what kind of sister one had. Jack stared at his brother, and gradually subsided into his buttered muffin again, and said nothing.

Gene was frowning thoughtfully. There was nothing about his countenance to indicate that he had not attended divine service every Sabbath of his life.

"Why, I'm not just sure but they've changed the hour. Is it ten or eleven, Dad? Seems to me somebody said something about changing the hour."

"It's likely eleven, then," said Elsie not seeming to notice. "Most of the city churches have it at eleven now, though ours was quarter of. You're all going with me, of course. I couldn't think of going the first time into a strange church, you know, without a full body-guard. I hope you don't sit away up front. I'd hate to have to go up front the first Sunday."

"Well, I haven't been going to church much lately," began the father. "Gene, here, 'll take you, or Jack."

"Why, of course they will, both of them; but I want you to go, too," declared Elsie. "We're all going together this first Sunday, no matter what happens. I don't want to feel homesick on Sunday, and it will take you all to keep me from it in church. There is no place where one feels homesick, you know, like a strange church!"

They looked at her in astonishment and dismay. They searched in their minds for their feeble arguments against this sudden family invasion of the staid old Morningside church that had paid no attention to them for the last five years; but in the end Elsie had her way. Somehow, when it came right down to it, they couldn't bear to let that sweet girl know that they had utterly given up religion. *Girls* ought to have religion, of course. They needed it for some vague reason, and it wouldn't do to shock her. So they went, every man of them, dressed up in the finest they had, with many a mental resolve to have better things on hand for another such unexpected excursion into the fashionable world.

At a quarter of eleven they issued forth from the house, father, daughter, and two sons, walking proudly together. The boys walked behind, with many admiring glances at the slender girl in her pretty suit and hat. If they *had* to go to church, at least no one else had a better-looking sister than they had. They made a show of picking a thread from her shoulder and jumping to pick up her handkerchief when she dropped it, and anyone could see they were almost ready to burst with pride over her looks.

The minister noticed the newcomers, and came down after the service to speak to them. It had perhaps never occurred to him before to go in search of this hopeless-looking man and his wild sons. They seemed far more impossible to win than the heathen on some distant shore. But now that they had come of their own accord he was glad to see them, and made them feel it. The father accepted his hearty hand-shake with a dumb wonder, and said little. This coming back into a world which had known him and his wife long years ago was a terribly shaking experience. He could think of little to say. He stood back respectfully quiet while Elsie said pleasant things to the minister, and told him where she had been attending church and that she had come now to live in her father's house. Somehow it gave him a great sense of comfort to hear her make that statement in the presence of others. Before it had seemed like a wonderful dream that might slip away at any time and leave the blank, dull loneliness again.

The brothers looked like wild things at bay when the minister came down the aisle toward them, and Jack would have bolted then and there but that it was too late.

They shook hands a trifle stiffly, as if they were not sure of the minister whether he were enemy or friend. They stood with alert, glittering gaze fixed steadily on him to see whether he gave Elsie the deference due her, or whether he let the fact that she belonged to them affect in the slightest his treatment of her. They had the attitude of being there to protect her and of barely tolerating his presence. Elsie, glancing at them lovingly, was proud of their gentlemanly bearing. She wondered whether the minister's genial smile would not win them. She liked him at once herself.

She did not say much about the church service on the way home. She had the feeling that she must go slowly with regard to church, and let them praise it if they would. And presently she was rewarded. Jack, walking behind with his brother, remarked:

"He seems to be a pretty good sort of guy," referring to the minister; and the father assented with unusual interest:

"Yes, that was a good sermon he gave us. It was all true what he said, too. Seemed as if he was preaching right to me."

"I guess he's a pretty good sort," added Gene. "I hear folks around town talk that way. You know he hasn't been here but a couple of months or so."

On the whole, Elsie was well satisfied with her morning's experiment, and sat down to dinner feeling that matters were doing well.

I wonder, is it true that whenever we congratulate ourselves that things are moving well there always comes along something to upset and spoil them? Is it a part of the work of the devil to watch for our complacency, and bring us face to face with something unpleasant right then and there?

However that may be, the thought had hardly escaped Elsie's consciousness before there came a sound of footsteps at the front door, and there was a loud call for Jack, as of one accustomed to such unceremonious entrances.

Jack leaped as if he had some kind of an electrical contrivance attached to him. The conversation seemed suspended in mid-air while he went to the door. There was a moment's low growl outside the vestibule, and then Jack returned, flinging down his napkin and snatching up his cap from the hall table with one and the same movement.

"I gotta beat it. So-long."

"O Jack!" came from Elsie with a wail of apprehension. "You haven't finished your dinner, and there's an awfully nice dessert, a new one."

"Can't help it," said Jack with a half-wistful look back at his plate, which was only half cleared. "I gotta go. The fellas were here twice for me this morning. I forgot all about it. Had this date for two weeks. Awful sorry, Elsie. You save me some, won't you?"

"But Jack!" said Elsie, her eyes suddenly filling with disappointed tears which she hadn't in the least summoned. "This is my first Sunday, and I thought we'd have such a nice time together."

"Gee! Elsie, I didn't go to do it. I tell you I had this date for two weeks back, and I *gotta* go. I'll get back as quick as I can."

"Will you be back by four o'clock? I wanted you and Gene to take me for a walk."

"I'll try," said Jack weakly, slamming the door hard to keep out the sound of Elsie's disappointed protest. He knew he couldn't get back. He was going on a thirty-mile jaunt in an automobile with some girls and fellows, and he knew it would be late before he could possibly return. He sneaked out the door and sprang into the car in three strides, his conscience and his stomach both protesting; yet he felt bound to go. He didn't have the nerve to back out. He knew perfectly well there were other fellows Bob Lowe could have asked to go with him. He didn't particularly want to go, hadn't wanted to much when he made the engagement, except for the ride, and to "pass the time away." But it was the way of the fellows, and he couldn't get out of it. They would "kid the life out of him" if he stayed home because his sister had come.

The little broken group at the table ate their dinner disconsolately after his departure.

"He'd no business going!" declared Gene. "It's that Bob Lowe. He's always carting Jack off somewhere. He's a lazy good-for-nothing himself, and he's always getting Jack into every fool scheme he can."

"Where do they go? What kind of a fellow is he?" Elsie was trying to conceal her disappointment and not spoil the day for the others.

"Oh, I don't know. They go off to see some girls or visit some fellows in the city. I never knew Bob to have anything worth while in view. He just fools. He doesn't even work. His father lets him do just as he pleases, lets him drive the car whenever he likes, and doesn't make him go to work. He's got some money, and Bob is going to spend it."

"Does he drink?"

Elsie asked the question in a low tone, a desperate fear pulling at her heart. What if Jack were in that danger?

"I don't know, I suppose so," answered Gene crossly. Something in his expression made his sister think he did know, only he didn't want to say.

She took a long breath, and tried to dismiss the subject and smile; but the father sat, thoughtfully looking out of the window and sighing now and then, with the regret of one who sees it is too late to undo the past. After dinner he went and sat in the big chair by himself with a newspaper spread before him, but he did not read. He was looking into the past and seeing where he might have led his sons by a different road.

Elsie wandered to the piano, and Gene sat near by, watching and listening. At first they tried to sing; but they missed Jack's voice, and somehow the fervor died out of the singing. Then Elsie began to play hymns and bits of variations, then a snatch of a Chopin nocturne, a strain of Handel's "Largo," a touch of Grieg's "Morning," anything that came into her troubled mind, while she watched and waited for the brother who, she instinctively knew, was not coming for a long time.

It became four o'clock, and half past; and then Eugene suggested that they take a walk. He said Jack would not be home till late that night; he never was back early when he went with Bob Lowe.

Elsie sighed, cast a troubled glance at her father, who was asleep in his chair, and finally yielded.

They walked out a long, quiet street that led to the cemetery. Perhaps neither of them realized where they were going until they came to it; and then Elsie, looking up with quick understanding of her surroundings, though it was long since she had been there, said impulsively:

"Let us go in, Gene. Can you find mother's grave?"

Standing on the bare brown hillside beside the grave, looking down to the little brook that rippled below in the late afternoon sunshine, looking up through the bare branches overhead to the autumn sky, a strange silence came over them. It seemed as if the two so long separated had all at once come close to the mother who was gone, and understood her cares and wishes.

"It seems to me I can remember that she worried about you a great deal, Gene. She was so anxious for you to grow up a good man and strong, she used to say." Elsie broke the silence without realizing what she was going to do.

"I know," said the brother, looking off quickly to the west where heavy purple clouds raggedly bound with gold gave hint of the coming sunset. Then hoarsely, reluctantly, after a minute, "She would be worried about Jack now, I suppose."

Elsie had no words to answer at once, but she laid her hand on her brother's arm.

"Couldn't we help—couldn't we try to do for him—

what she would have done if she had lived?" she asked at length.

"Perhaps," said the boy, strangely moved. "He ought to get away from the factories!" he said fiercely after a minute. "It's no place for him. He's too young. You don't know what it's like over there."

Elsie was still for some minutes. When she spoke again, her voice was stronger, as if she had come to some decision.

"He ought to go back to school, Gene. He *must* go to college!"

"He'll never do it." The brother shook his head sadly.

"He would if *you* did."

They had turned and were walking back to the street now, and the golden light of the setting sun was streaming forth from between two purply-black ragged clouds, and lit the girl's face. Her eyes were stern with a holy determination, and her lips were set. Her brother saw there was real purpose in her words and she meant to fight every inch of the way. He looked at her, and conviction stole into his heart. Yes, Jack would probably go to college if he went, and would never go unless he did. Yet it seemed just as impossible to him as ever that he at the age of twenty-three should presume to think of going to college; but still there was at least this one good reason for it, that if he went his brother might also be induced to go.

Elsie talked about it all the way back, but her brother said very little beyond shaking his head once or twice and telling her it was impossible. Nevertheless, she went on talking, and declared she meant to find out about classes and entrance examinations the very next day. Her brother only laughed, and told her she had the perseverance of the saints, and didn't she know he couldn't possibly go to college?

Then they went in, and Elsie with her brother's help made delicate little sandwiches and cocoa, and got out an apple pie and some chocolate cake and peaches. All the time they were eating she kept listening and watching for Jack, her heart jumping at every noise.

And all at once he came, sullenly, noisily, wearily, she thought, slamming the door and flinging down his hat and coat. He was cold and cross and hungry, and "sore as the deuce," as he expressed it. Bob Lowe had kidded him all the way over about going to church; and, when they reached their destination, the girls had gone off with another fellow, naturally, as he had not arrived when he said he would; and Bob Lowe was very sore indeed, and laid the blame wholly on Jack. Things grew so uncomfortable on the way back that Jack had parted from Bob as soon as they came near the city lines, and had come home on the trolley; and the whole affair had not improved Jack's temper. Moreover, Jack knew that he had been rude and impolite to his sister, and he was consequently more rude and impolite to make up for it. On the whole, Elsie judged it unwise to suggest going to church again that night, and instead covered Jack up on the couch, and sang and read to the three for an hour.

She was very weary and sick at heart when she went up to her room that night, also worried about Jack. Half impatiently she told herself as she lay down that, if the boys were going to get tired of staying at home with her, it would be useless for her to remain here. And then immediately came the thought that it was just because of the need for some one to lure them to stay home that she had come, and she must not mind a few discouragements.

IT WAS not easy to arise a whole hour earlier in the morning than she was accustomed to do, and, when Elsie looked out of her window on a gray day with sullen clouds in the background, she sighed and wondered whether after all she had not made a terrible mistake. Somehow in the gray of the cold early morning the little rose room in its daintiness did not make its appeal as it did in the brightness of day or of electric light.

Nevertheless, she managed to keep her face cheerful and make the breakfast a pleasant time to remember as each went his way for thc day; and when she had finally seated herself in the trolley, she was able to smile clear down into her heart and look at things bravely. She was going to town to get some circulars and a catalogue of the university to-day. She was going to call up the dean and ask a lot of questions. She had written them all down on a card so that she would forget nothing. If it were a possible thing, she meant to get Eugene to start in at the university. There was no reason at all why he shouldn't. It might be a fight to get him to go, but Elsie felt the joy of the battle, and the day began to look good to her. By the time she arrived at her friend's home she was in excellent spirits. A few questions to the girl whose young brother had just entered the university made her feel still more hopeful, and her talk with the dean of the university sent her spirits soaring hopefully. The thing she proposed for her brother was not nearly so impossible a matter as she had feared. When she went back to Morningside she was fortified with much information; and she could hardly wait until supper was over before she began at her brother.

But Eugene had been through a long day of thinking. In imagination he had faced all sorts of possible situations in an unknown university, and he had firmly fixed his stakes that he would never, never go. Elsie found she had to do her work all over again. Once she was almost in despair and came near breaking down. She had so hoped to get him to go down and see the dean at once, but she saw now it would be impossible. However, he was deeply moved, and finally promised her he would think about it again.

All that week the battle went on, Elsie plying him at night with new arguments, new information, begging, fairly praying him to waste no more time, and Eugene coming home every night equally fortified with arguments and stubbornness against it. It got to be quite interesting, almost as good as a football game, Jack declared, while he sat and listened, putting in a word now on one side, now on the other. The discussion was not doing Jack any harm. He was learning a lot of things about education and universities, and his interest was being aroused.

Even the father took a hand in the conversation now and then.

Toward the end of the summer Elsie almost gave up hope. One could see by her eyes and by her nervous, eager voice that she had the thing deeply at heart. Eugene was greatly touched that she seemed to care so much, and questioned within himself haughtily, was it because she was ashamed of him as he was? Did she fear her fine friends would come out to see her, and turn away from her because of her ignorant brother? For a whole day this thought held him in its sullen thrall; then suddenly it occurred to him that perhaps he *was* a disgrace to her, that undoubtedly he did not know much, and must appear crude beside the men she had been used to; and a longing desire to be different sprang up within him, and a gratitude to his sister for caring what he was. It was so that he came to realize that Elsie was doing all this out of genuine concern for him. She had no call to come out to Morningside. She might have stayed in town and enjoyed herself, and let her brothers go to grass. It needn't have troubled her what they were.

At last one night he stayed awake half the night to come to a conclusion about it. In the morning he astounded the family by announcing at the breakfast-table that he was done with the factory and meant to stay home that morning and get ready to go to the university. He would go down and see that dean; and, if they would take his credits, he would make a stab at it anyway for a while. If he wasn't too stupid, he would stick and graduate. If he found he couldn't hold his own after a month's trial, he would go back to work, and nobody need say a word about it, for he would be done with it forever.

Elsie in her delight almost upset the coffee-pot to rush from her place and put her arms around his neck. Jack sat back forgetful of the buckwheat cakes and maple-syrup, and looked at his brother in a kind of wonder, as if he had never quite known him before.

There was something strong and refreshing about

Gene's manner. He seemed to shut his lips a more decisive way, and his very smile was as of a creature made over. He seemed to be seeing things from a different point of view, to have grown up overnight. Jack continued to sit and watch him, wholly unaware that he was doing so, a puzzled, half-pitying expression on his face.

Elsie offered to go to the university with her brother and introduce him to some people she knew there, but he gently and firmly declined her services. Somehow he seemed to have developed a self-confidence and strength that astonished them all. The father sat and stared at his son, and said as he got up to take his old hat and go out to the trolley:

"Well, Gene, your mother would have been pleased. I guess you're doing the right thing."

Gene was gone all day. Elsie spent much time going to the window and watching every trolley to see whether he was coming, and she grew anxious and restless, wishing she had insisted upon accompanying him, after all. There was no telling what might switch him away from his purpose if he found things different from his expectations.

The fireplace created a pleasant diversion, getting itself finished; and, when the men were done and gone, she built up a beautiful fire and had it ready to light when the family should return.

Gene was the last to arrive, and came in from the trolley just as they had about made up their minds to sit down to the table without him. They greeted him as though he had been lost, and then were silent under his changed, radiant look.

"Well, I've had some time!" he said, beaming round upon them all. "Just wait till I wash up a bit, and I'll tell you."

"Well, you've certainly made a day of it. Just take your

time, old man," shouted Jack, as his brother disappeared up the stairs in three bounds.

Eugene plunged into his story at once when he came down.

You see I found Tod Hopkins down there, ran into him the first thing while I was inquiring the way to the office; and he just carried me around all day everywhere, introduced me to all the profs and the fellows, and helped me mark out my course. Tod Hopkins, you remember him, Jack; played half-back on our football team the first year we had it? Yes, sure! He's in the university, a senior. Sure, he's a senior; three years since he left here; and you better believe it was some help to me, too. A senior seems to know about everything, and be able to go everywhere and do anything. What he says goes, at least, that's the way it is with Tod. Mebbe he wasn't glad to see me. Slapped me on the back, and introduced me to the football team. Told them I used to be the best high-school quarter-back he ever saw, and a lot of bull like that; and then he took me around to his frat house for dinner. It's some house. You ought to see it. There's an Oriental rug on that floor that must have cost thousands of dollars. It's like that big one we saw hanging up on the wall in the store, Jack. I'll take you down to see it sometime!"

"You'll take me down!" exclaimed his brother. "Did they give you free range of their frat house?"

Eugene looked proudly around at them.

"I'm as good as pledged," he said radiantly. Then he caught a troubled look in Elsie's eye. "Oh, you needn't worry, Elsie, they don't drink in this frat, not a one of them. They aren't that kind. Tod's president this year, and they're mostly students that are working their way, and honor men. They've got a few rich ones, but they are all real men."

"Is that why they took you in?" asked his brother dryly, albeit his eyes were shining appreciatively.

Gene laughed. He was too happy to mind his brother's sarcasm.

"But how about your studies?" questioned Elsie anxiously. Surely Gene hadn't spent his whole day getting in with the boys and going to a frat house!

"Oh, they're all right"—as if he hadn't thought to mention a minor detail like that. "I struck the dump just in time to catch Prexie and the dean. They wanted my credits; so I called up Higginson, our superintendent here in Morningside. I was lucky enough to find him home, too; and he talked to them over the phone, gave them a pretty good line of talk about me; said I was bright, and all that dope, and he was glad I had decided to go on with my studies—as if *I* ever *studied* much!—and Prexie took it all in, and said I could go ahead and not wait till the credits got there; it was all right. Tod took me round, and I got signed up. Tod knocked me down to some of the fellows in the freshman English and math.

"I'm taking the engineering course, you know; that's what I've always wanted to do."

"Not for mine!" interrupted Jack. "No sir! If I ever go to college, I'm going to specialize in chemistry. There's big money in chemistry in the next few years, believe me."

Elsie's eyes shone, but she said nothing.

"Yes, I guess there is," said Gene; "but it isn't in my line. I've always wanted to study engineering. The shop work's what I'm going to like. I went over to the shop with the fellows this afternoon, and I sure am going to like that. There's one fellow making an automobile from beginning to end. Some job! Oh, but it's a great place! I wish you could see it."

Eugene had not talked so much nor so well for years. His father looked at him in wonder. He was like a new being. Jack was silent with admiration. College life loomed large before his eyes, and his determination against it for himself had suffered a severe blow. Already he was thinking of what he would do if he ever got into the university, and he sighed involuntarily as he reflected on his wasted years in the high school and how he might have been ready to enter without any trouble by this time, if he had used his opportunities.

All together that was a most interesting evening, for there seemed no end to the things Eugene had to tell about the university; and, when he reached the end of a tale, he began and told it over again with new touches. It was as if he had suddenly broken away from his routine of work and taken a hasty trip to Europe, he had seen and heard so much and it had stirred him so deeply. Elsie was quite content to sit and listen. Even the new fireplace was almost forgotten while they lingered around the dining-table long after the maid had cleared it off and washed the dishes.

At last Elsie remembered and slipping into the other room, touched a match to her fire, and called the rest of them; and for an hour or two they sat in the firelight, seeing visions of a future wherein new ambitions and comforts had a part.

It came to Elsie's consciousness once while she was sitting there listening to her brother's talk about the university, watching the firelight play on the content of her father's worn face, and the dreamy wistfulness of Jack's eyes, that she had entirely forgotten about her aunt and the home she had left behind. It came to her with a pang, as if she had done something wrong to forget them, who had been so kind and dear to her. Yet how could she mourn about going into this new, wonderful place where there was so much to be done and nobody but herself to do it?

It was all very wonderful, but after all quite exhausting; and, when she went up to her room that night, she found that she had quite as many things to worry about, if she chose to let them bother her, as she had to rejoice over. For instance, there was that frat. She had heard a lot about fraternities. What if this should be one of those that led young men to destruction? Of course Eugene would think it was all right if his friend said so, but he couldn't judge all about it until he got into it. She wished he would wait until he could be sure what kind of boys he was getting in with. Then there was that "Tod" fellow, some old friend of his high school days from Morningside. He might be the wildest fellow imaginable. How unfortunate that Eugene should have met him right at the start! She had wanted to introduce Eugene to a few young men she knew who would steer him into the right crowd, and now it was too late! He would always stick to that "Tod" fellow in spite of anything she might say. On the whole, she had laid out a good job of worry for herself that night; and, if she hadn't been so very tired, she might have stayed awake all night and attended to it. But as it was she had worked hard all day, and nature got the better of her. She slept soundly and late.

Elsie had succeeded better than her fondest hopes in getting her family of grown-up boys to go to church. Always one of them accompanied her and very often all three went. It was on one of these occasions that Elsie saw Cameron Stewart again.

It was after church that they were introduced to him. The minister was at the bottom of it. He was delighted to see that whole new family in church again, and he came straight down from the pulpit as soon as he reasonably could, to speak to them. It was altogether natural that he should also speak to the young stranger who had been to church once or twice before. It was also natural that he should turn and introduce the young people.

As Elsie acknowledged the introduction, she wondered vaguely where she had seen that man before and what there was about his eyes that seemed so familiar. When she looked up a second time to clear the fleeting memory, she found him looking intently at her.

"I think we have met before, Miss Hathaway," said the young man with a pleasant smile, "our mutual friend Professor Bowen—" But Elsie heard no more. A flood of memory brought the color to her cheeks, as suddenly she knew that he was also the young man of the trolley who had seen her crying one night and she was overwhelmed with embarrassment. But the minister created a diversion with a question to Eugene.

"You are employed at Brainerd's, Mr. Hathaway, I think you said?"

"My brother has entered the university, Doctor Baker." Elsie's clear voice brought out the information with a ring of pleasure. The echo of it sent a flush of pride and pleasure into Gene's face as he bowed slightly in acknowledgment of the truth of what she had said. The minister's eyes lighted, and he looked at the young man with new respect, which Gene could not help feeling. There was also a sudden quick light in the eyes of Cameron Stewart as he looked first at the brother and then back to the sister keenly. Had the girl done all that in the short time she had been living at home, or was it a work of months past?

"Oh!" said the minister. "Then it is your other brother, or has he too entered the university?"

"Not yet," said Elsie with a daring smile; "but we hope he will be able to enter next fall."

"Ah! That is good. I congratulate you. There is nothing like college days. I wish I could go back and have mine over again. But you are still at Brainerd's? I mention it because there is a young fellow, a stranger in this part of the country, the son of an old friend of mine, who has just gone over there to work. I should be glad if you will look him up and be a little friendly. His name is Bently, Hugh Bently. If you come across him, just give him a word now and then. I'm sure he will be glad of it."

There was that in the minister's tone that implied that Jack was not only a friend of his and a part of the working force of this church, but also that a word from him would be an honor to any stranger to whom it might be granted. And behold, Jack went forth from that church, not only publicly committed to entering the university in the fall, for he had smiled assent to Elsie's declaration, but a commissioned messenger from the minister to a stranger who needed a kind word. Jack swelled along quite set up with the honor of it. On the whole, Elsie was very happy that day, in spite of her embarrassment before that obnoxious young man. But she didn't have much time or thought to give to Cameron.

THERE was nothing easy about the life that Elsie had chosen. To get up an hour earlier than she had been accustomed to do in the city that she might eat breakfast with her family and catch an early car, often studying her lessons all the way into the city; to forget that there existed such things as symphony concerts and teas and dinners and receptions and automobile-rides and the numberless rounds of joys that had been hers; and to rush straight home from school to see that the house was in order and cheerful, and perhaps prepare some dainty for dessert that the clumsy new maid could not yet master; to give her evenings to studying out intricate problems in college algebra, and to correcting and advising about "themes," and to coaxing Jack to lie on the sofa and let her read Shakespeare, or *The Lady of the Lake*, or *Ivanhoe*, or some other classic which she had carefully discovered belonged in the list of college-examination subjects; to bear sudden nameless fears of her own, and strange erratic actions on the part of the three men who were her household; to sing to them, play to them, laugh for them whenever she saw they needed it; all this was not easy. It was "no cinch," as Jack would say.

Sometimes she was weary enough to throw herself on her little white bed and cry; yet always, when she got near to it, the beauty of that rose-satin eider-down quilt would cry out to her, the silver frames on the wall, the silver-backed hair-brushes on the bureau, would reflect to her the love her brothers had given her, and their need and longing for her; and she would be constrained to rise and go on again with her burdens.

There was one thing she did not know, and that was that Cameron Stewart was watching her, taking notes of what manner of girl she was, and very much approving her. For Cameron Stewart had been transferred to the Eastern office of his firm, and was making his home for the present out at Morningside with the friend whom he had called upon the day of the memorable ride on the trolley when he had seen Elsie crying.

But one morning coming down the street on his way to the station he saw Elsie standing at the corner by her father's house, waiting for the trolley. Following an impulse, he took the trolley also. Thereafter, whenever he was out at Morningside, he went into town on that particular trolley for a little experimenting showed him that Elsie always went in at the same time.

Yet he scarcely ever got even a bow for his trouble, for she walked to the nearest seat and plunged into her book which seemed to be absorbing; and she seldom had eyes for those about her. The first two or three times he was sure she did not recognize that she had ever seen him before; but he soon began to realize that she was avoiding him with intention. She never sat down near him if she could find another seat. Yet he liked her for it, and he usually planned to sit so that her clear profile would be outlined in his range of vision. He liked to see the sweet seriousness with which she performed her work, and to watch the business-like little hand that set down decided figures and characters in her note-book.

But somehow he did not seem to get any nearer to an acquaintance with her than if he had gone into town on the train instead of the trolley. Nevertheless, he continued to start early and patronize the trolley.

But one evening Cameron Stewart came boldly over to the house with a great armful of the most wonderful, glowing, out-of-door chrysanthemums, pink, white, gold, and crimson. He looked like a florist as he stood at the door and waited to be admitted; and the maid let him into the parlor where the fire was flickering sleepily away and the old cat, now robbed of her gauntness, sat sleek and neat, with her paws folded on the hearth and a contented purr rumbling softly in her breast. He drew a sigh of relief as he entered and looked around. He would not have liked to have that room be the conventional "best room," crude, stiff, and ostentatious. He had felt that it would be different; but he had not been prepared for this room, this cozy, artistic, homelike refuge from the cares of the world; for that was what it looked like.

The big stone fireplace was finished with a stone shelf over which a latticed mirror gave the room a cozy distance. Each side of the chimney low bookcases were finished with casement windows, their lattice matching that over the fireplace. The firelight glowed over the gilt letters of the books and showed up their covers of crimson and blue and green. The old brass andirons that Elsie had found in the attic reflected the gleam of the fire.

A comfortable couch draped in a Bagdad rug, with big crimson pillows piled at the head, was rolled out into the room in the neighborhood of the fireplace.

All the other furniture in the room, the chairs, the music-cabinet, the big table with the pretty lamp, even the piano, seemed set in a grouping toward the fireplace, as though it were the heart, the altar, of the room. The walls were of a soft neutral tint, and the old crayon and oil portraits that hung about when Elsie came had been banished. Only two or three good pictures were left. Some small, inexpensive Oriental rugs were scattered about here and there, and the whole room looked a real "living-room," not in any sense a parlor or drawing-room. It breathed its coziness and welcome as one came in.

The pleasantness of it entered the young man's soul with a fine surprise. He had brought his flowers dubiously, wondering whether they would not be going into an alien atmosphere which it was doubtful whether they could do much in the way of glorifying. Now he realized that they belonged here and would glow out from the dusky quietness, catching the gleam of the firelight and blending exquisitely with the place.

Then Elsie came into the room, a fitting mistress of the place in her bright crimson house-gown, a little glow on her cheeks from a brisk walk she had just taken to the store for something that was needed for supper, her brown hair ruffled into little rebellious curls around her face. She came forward with startled surprise in her face; which held him at a distance in spite of his strong resolve to break down the wall between them: He had risen as she came in the room and held out his flowers.

"These flowers were just running riot in the yard," he said, "and crying out to be picked. Our folks are all away for a week and you are the only person I know in Morningside. Will you take them and enjoy them?" What could Elsie do then but be gracious?

She took the flowers from him, and made him sit down while she began to arrange them in jars and a big brass bowl on the stone mantel. They seemed to be just the touch the room needed to make it perfect. Cameron Stewart looked from her to the flowers, and was thinking how they seemed to belong together, when she turned with a pretty little gesture of delight and said quaintly,

"Oh, don't they look happy?"

He laughed joyously. The phrase was so unusual and so fitting.

"They do!" said he. "I was just trying to get hold of a phrase, but you have struck it exactly; they look happy. Flowers have to have the right environment to look their best, just as people do; and I believe this room was just made to set off these flowers. Everything seems to 'look happy' in here."

He cast his eyes about admiringly, and let them rest for a moment lingeringly on the slim girl standing beside the flowers.

He did not stay more than a minute or two that first time. It was almost dinner-time. He could smell delicious odors faintly stealing through from the regions of the kitchen, and he knew he had no excuse to remain; but, as he was going out, he looked toward the piano, and noticed a volume of Beethoven's sonatas lying open on the rack.

"You play!" he said with a sudden lighting of his eyes.

"A little," said Elsie. "Of course I don't have much time these days for practising."

"I wish I might come over and listen sometime." There was a wistfulness in his voice, and what could she do but give him permission? although she warned him that he would be sure to be disappointed if he came.

As he went out the door, Eugene came up the steps, a pile of books under his arm, and stopped his merry whistle at sight of the stranger.

Stewart put out his hand.

"You're just getting home from the university? Then you come home every night? What a privilege!"

"Think so? Well, 'tis a privilege since my sister's home," admitted the young man with a gallant glance at the girl. "But one misses a lot of things not living down there."

"Yes, a few, perhaps; but one misses a lot of things not being here, I should suppose; and I can tell you a university life gets mighty tiresome when one's had it steadily without anything else. I've had ten years of school without any home to go to; so I know. Well, I won't keep you. I can sniff a mighty good dinner waiting for you, so good-night."

"He isn't so bad when you see him close," affirmed Eugene as he followed his sister into the house. "Ten years! Good-night!"

EUGENE'S work at the university was going very well. He was taking hold of things with a vim, and seemed to be happy in his new environment. Elsie had not been long in discovering from her friend, Professor Bowen, that Tod Hopkins was no fearful bugbear to be dreaded. He was the best beloved of the university, the idol alike of both faculty and student body, the finest, strongest, brainiest, best all-around student, athlete, and everything else that the university had enrolled in years.

"And he's awfully religious, too," the principal had added. "Gives talks to the boys on all sorts of ethical subjects, and sometimes holds prayer meetings, actually *prays!* Doesn't it sound strange? And yet the boys say it isn't at all incongruous."

Instantly all Elsie's fears of Tod Hopkins vanished. If he was that kind of fellow, Heaven be praised! She would do all she could to further Eugene's love for him. And when after a little her brother came home with a mysterious little silver symbol embedded in the fabric of his vest, and announced that he was "pledged," she said not a word against fraternities, but bent her energies toward furthering her brother's plans.

"Our frat puts no end of stress on marks. We want to get the highest average of any frat this year," he announced one day after he had been duly initiated and had exchanged the symbol of mystery for a pin of enamel and gold. Then Elsie openly rejoiced that her brother was a member. He was really studying hard. The mid-semester examinations were upon him, and now was the test whether he would be able to catch up with his class. She had been fearful lest he should get discouraged, but the blessed "frat" seemed to be behind him, cheering him on to success.

"Tod thinks I might stand a chance of getting on the scrub football team if I get through these all right," he announced one morning at breakfast. "There's a corker of an exam to-morrow in English lit, and I sha'n't have a minute to-day to study up, either. Have to be at shop work all the afternoon."

"Never mind," said Elsie, smiling. "I'll come home early, and go over the things, and pick out what you ought to concentrate on; and then this evening we'll go over them together. Professor Bowen says you can do twice as much in preparing for an examination if you have some system about your preparation instead of trying to cram all creation into your brain in one evening. You want to be sure of the stories of the books you've read, a general outline, and be ready to have some kind of opinion on the subject-matter of each. There'll be likely to be a few dates to get fixed in your mind, and I'll glance through things, and call your attention to any passages you'll be likely to have to locate or quote, so you can brush up on them. Don't you worry. I'll stick by you, and you'll get through all right."

"You're a trump, Elsie," said her brother, flashing a

look of appreciation toward her that sent her off to her school day with a warm and happy heart, and kept her thinking pleasantly, with real anticipation of the evening and how she could best help her brother.

Then at recess one of the girls came from the office with a message for her.

"Elsie, your cousin Katharine wants to speak with you at the telephone."

Elsie's heart beat wildly as she rose from her desk to go to the telephone. Not in all the weeks she had been away from her aunt's had there come a sign or word from any of them except her uncle. He had written her a comforting little note the first week of her absence, telling her that they were missing her greatly, but he was proud of her that she could follow in the way of duty. He also enclosed a substantial check, which he asked her to use for little things that she might find lacking in her home, things to which she had been accustomed lately, and which she might miss. He said he should be happier to think she had them. She had responded by a frank, loving letter thanking him fervently, accepting the check, as she knew he would want her to do, and be terribly hurt if she did not, and telling him what a dear, precious uncle he was and how glad she was he was her uncle.

She had also written to her aunt dutifully and pleasantly, hoping that she was forgiven for insisting on following her present course, but trying to make it plain that she still felt even more strongly that it was the path of right, and begging that they would come out and see for themselves.

Not one word had she received in reply.

Later she wrote to each of her cousins, but nothing came in answer. The fourth week she wrote to her aunt again, and tried once more to make plain what she was attempting to do for her home, her father and brothers; but still nothing came of it. After that she settled down to the inevitable, and with many a tear tried to resign herself to the break with those who were so near and dear to her. She knew of course that they were away at their seashore cottage. But they had plenty of time to write.

Now, when the sudden, unexpected message came that Katharine was at the telephone waiting to speak with her, her limbs trembled beneath her, and things in the schoolroom seemed confused and whirling for just an instant. But she rallied, smilingly thanked the messenger, and went to the phone. Her hand trembled a little as she took up the receiver; but she managed to control her voice and say, "Hello!"

Yes, it was Katharine's voice, but cold and distant, almost condescending in its reserve.

"Is that you, Elsie? Mamma wished me to phone for her and say that she has arranged to have some of your friends here this evening, and she would like you to come directly here from school and remain all night."

"O Katharine! How dear of Auntie!" exclaimed Elsie, her heart all aglow with warmth, utterly forgetful of the cold tone in which the invitation was uttered. "But I'm *so* sorry I can't come! It would be just beautiful, and I'm perfectly hungry to see you all; but it's just impossible to-night. You see I promised Eugene I'd be at home early to help him with something—"

Katharine's cold voice cut in on her explanation.

"Mamma has not been at all well since you left us in that unceremonious style, and you certainly owe it to her to do as she asks, especially when she has planned something for your pleasure. Telephone your brother you cannot come. You can help him another time.

Mamma needs you now, and the other people are all invited."

"I'm so sorry, dear!" wailed Elsie. "Anything else in the world, almost, I could put off; I would find some way to do it; but this is very important. You see Eugene—"

"Oh, very well," interrupted Katharine again, "of course you have a perfect *right* to choose whom you will please, regardless of how much you hurt your best friends. I will tell Mamma what you say. Good-by."

"But Katharine!" Elsie's voice broke in a sob. Katharine had hung up!

The bell was ringing for the close of recess, and Elsie dragged herself back to her desk, and she struggled to regain her self-control; but she looked fairly stricken all the rest of the morning, and one of the teachers at noon-time had told her she looked wretched, asked whether she had a headache, and advised her to go and lie down.

It was not until almost time for the afternoon session to close that it suddenly came to her that life was all made up of sorrowful things. There would be those in her home who would be watching for her and glad to see her. It was hard to have her aunt and cousins take things this way, and treat her like an alien and a stranger merely because she had seen her duty and gone back to her father's house; but that house was growing more dear every day, and her father and brothers were obviously doing all they could in their poor way to welcome her and make her happy. She would not despond. She would forget the sorrowful, and turn to the bright. How thankful she ought to be that Eugene wanted her, that he was really in college and making good, that he was eager to study for that examination, and that she could help him.

She straightaway put out of her mind the uncomfortable happening, and set to work on what she had promised to do for her brother. She selected a few books from the school library to take home with her, and worked at them diligently all the way out to Morningside. She arranged to have dinner on the table the minute her father and the boys came home, so that no time need be lost in the evening; and she put on her prettiest house-frock, and went down smilingly, smothering a sigh over the merry company who were probably assembling at her aunt's dinner-table at about that time. She had chosen. She had put her hand to the plough, and she would not look back.

While they were at dinner, Bob Lowe arrived at the front door, and called for Jack. Elsie's troubled look caught the boy's eyes, and he smiled back at her.

"Don't you worry, kid," he whispered as he went by her to go out and speak to his friend. "I'm not going. That couch looks good to me if you're going to read."

She nodded brightly. She certainly was going to read, and some of the things she would read would be along lines that would help him to get ready for his examinations next fall, but she didn't mean to let him know it. She meant to make it interesting to him and hold him at home; that was all; and a thrill of gladness shot through her. Here was a reason why she should have been at home to-night, another justification for her answer to Katharine's invitation. It had troubled her so all the afternoon that she had had to seem ungrateful and unkind to her aunt. But now, here, if she had been away this evening, Jack would most certainly have gone out with Bob Lowe; and that was never a thing to be desired.

It was a difficult task she had set herself, to combine an interesting evening of reading with a thorough review of half a semester's work in an English literature class, but she managed to do it after a fashion, and for two whole hours she read and commented and handed out facts for Eugene to set down in a list which he should look over and memorize on his way to the university in the morning.

They began as soon as dinner was over, the father dozing over his paper by the big table in the lamplight for a time, and going up early to bed. By nine o'clock they had gone briefly over the ground that the class had covered in the ten weeks the semester's work had begun; and Eugene flung down his pencil with a yawn, and threw himself back in the chair.

"That's enough, Elsie. I guess I'll manage to scrub through with all that crammed in my brain. I'll go over some of those things again in the morning. There's just one more thing I want to do to-night, and I guess I'd better quit this and get at it, for it's likely to last me all night. There's a tough old nut of a problem in algebra lesson for to-morrow; and none of the fellows had got it so far when I left this afternoon. I'd like to get it if I could. It would give me a drag with the prof, and make him give me good marks all year. They say it counts a lot what you get the first semester. They sort of get in the habit of marking you that way. Besides, I need a good mark or two to carry me through; and, if I am recommended by the math prof, I'll likely be asked on the basket-ball team. There's even a chance I might get on the varsity team, though it's not likely, but they're short one man, and they've spoken to me. It's up to me to get in with that prof, for what he says goes in athletics. If he says you're not up in your marks enough to play, it's no use trying anything else. But you don't know much about college algebra, do you?"

"Well, I might work at it and see if I get the same results you do," said Elsie smothering a yawn and sitting up bravely. She had had a hard day, and felt a sudden goneness in her back and head. But she drew a pad toward her, and got out her pencil, setting down the problem as Eugene read it aloud to her. Jack lay on the couch, and annoyed the cat with a feather he had pulled from one of the cushions, tickling her nose and eyelashes and toes delicately, and enjoying her renewed surprise and vexed response to each effort.

They had not been working on the problem three minutes when the silence of the room was broken by a ring of the doorbell. Elsie and Eugene looked up annoyed; but Jack dragged himself alertly from his couch, and went to the door. He was ready now to go out for a while if Bob Lowe had returned for him. He had had his rest and felt refreshed.

BUT the visitor was not Bob Lowe, who would have beckoned Jack outside the door. This man stepped inside, and took off his motor-cap with an air of haste and eagerness.

"I hope I'm not interrupting," he said pleasantly, as he noticed the two at work around the table.

Under his breath Eugene was uttering an exclamation of extreme annoyance, though he rose politely enough. He began to figure out how he could take his problem and "beat it" upstairs.

"I've just dropped in to see whether you all wouldn't like to take a little spin with me in my new car. I really don't enjoy doing things alone. Besides, it's a glorious night. The moon is full, and is flooding everything with silver. What do you say? Will you all go?"

He looked from one to the other of them eagerly.

Jack's eyes were alight at once. "What kind is it?" he asked.

Elsie did some quick thinking. She saw thc eagerness in Jack's face, the sudden light and then gloom on

Eugene's, as he glanced back at the unfinished problem; and she made her resolve.

"You're very kind," she began with that quick lift of her chin that betokened decision. "It would be lovely to go, but Eugene and I have a tough proposition on hand in the shape of a tricky problem in algebra that has to be done for an eight-o'clock class to-morrow morning; so I guess we'll have to decline. I know Jack would love to go with you for a while, though."

The kind, keen eyes of Stewart were searching her face as she talked. He was trying to determine whether it was duty to her brother, or only an excuse.

"Indeed, Elsie, you're not going to stay home for me," declared Eugene, turning upon her quite blusteringly. "If anybody stays at home, it'll be me. But I won't! Let the old problem go hang. I couldn't get it anyway. Why worry?"

The visitor watched the chasing of pleased surprise, of real eagerness, and of final anxiety over the sensitive face of the girl, and was satisfied.

"What's the matter with our all tackling that problem first, and then taking the ride," he asked. "Come show me what it is. I used to be good at math when I was in college."

Before they could protest they were all settled down again around the table, while Jack went out to cover up the engine and look admiringly at the shining new machine standing alluringly in the moonlight with the long stretch of white road like a ribbon all ready for it to leap out upon. He was happy as a king to get a chance to ride in the new machine, one of the best and most expensive high-powered machines made.

When he sauntered back into the house impatiently to see whether the others were not ready, he found it all very still in the living-room, where three heads were bent over three respective papers, and three pencils were ciphering away like express trains.

Jack sat down in a big chair, and furtively studied the fellow.

Cameron Stewart had thrown off his fur-lined overcoat, and it trailed on the floor regardless of its richness. His hair was ruffled up quite unconventionally, and his brows were knit. His fingers worked swiftly with a sureness as if they were going a familiar way. Presently he looked up, and spoke to Eugene.

"Got any result yet?"

"A sort of one," said Gene gloomily.

"Let me see what you've done."

He reached out, and took Gene's paper, touching the rows of figures lightly as he ran down the lines.

"All right so far," he said with authority as though he were the author of the problem; "but why did you do this?"

"I don't know," answered Eugene lamely. "Guess because I'd tried everything else."

"Well, but what was it you wanted to find here? What were you after?"

"Why, a common denominator."

"Exactly. How do you do that? What's your rule?"

"Oh! Why! I certainly am a nut!"

He reached out for his paper, and began to figure again rapidly, the visitor watching him sharply and Elsie rising and looking over his shoulder, eager to find out where she had been wrong.

"That's right. Go on. You're on the right track," encouraged Stewart as Eugene's pencil hesitated at another crucial point.

Jack sat watching, a half wistful expression in his eyes. Would he ever be figuring away like that, understanding all that jargon? Not that he cared in the least for the figuring or the jargon, more than as it represented the shibboleth of the classic realms of the university, where one played football with a halo of knowledge about one's head.

"Well, there!" exclaimed Eugene at length, as his frantic figuring came to an end, and signs and symbols covered the entire sheet of paper. "Is that right? Gee! I believe it is! Where's that book? It belonged to a fellow in last year's class, and he had the answer written down. Hooray! Yes, it is. Thanks awfully, Stewart. If it hadn't been for you, I'd have been all night at it, and not got it then, unless Elsie got onto it. I certainly am obliged to you."

"Oh, I didn't do a thing but make you use your own brains," answered the visitor happily as he began to put on his overcoat again.

"Well, I guess that's about the size of it. You see I'm new at brain-work." Eugene's voice was slightly deferential. It had lost the contempt and conceit wherewith he had propped his own conscious lack. He had been made to see for the first time in a succession of years where he had been wrong, and a bit of real humility was pleasantly upon him. There is nothing that sits more pleasantly upon an arrogant young man than a sudden infusion of sincere humility and gratitude.

"You're all right, old fellow; you'll soon get on to it again," said Stewart, slapping him genially on the shoulder in a way that would have been resented by Eugene a short half-hour before. Now it warmed his heart with comradeship, the surprising comradeship of one who has proved himself a superior in something.

"Now for our ride!" said Stewart. "Bring plenty of wraps; the night is rather cool. I have two big, warm rugs."

Five minutes more, and they were out in the car,

leaping over the white road, the sharp, invigorating November air striking their faces refreshingly after their evening of hard work, and the moon paving the world with silver.

Out into the country they shot, past the lights of Morningside—the little inn, and the Country Club; past the golf links and the bridge where the creek slid silverly under; through lanes where bare branches met overhead and grave cedars whispered spicily; between fields of ghostly corn-shocks huddled in groups murmuring uncannily of better days; where mists rose in white wreaths over a swamp; with the lights of the distant city on one hand and the lights of the distant riverboats and lighthouses on the other hand, they rushed, quiet for the most part, happy with a kind of joy of new-found friendship that none of them could have explained.

Jack was in the front seat beside his host. He had gone there as a matter of course, with the eagerness of a boy who is bound to be at the point of greatest interest. It never occurred to him that Stewart might have preferred some one else. He simply located himself there without question.

Stewart would have enjoyed having Elsie beside him. He wanted to talk to her. Yet he reflected that, after all, this arrangement was better all around. So the conversation, what there was of it, became general, and delightful to all.

Jack and Stewart grew quite chummy over the machine, talking over its various good points, Stewart explaining several things that Jack had not understood before, and Jack in his turn giving an intelligent reason for so-and-so being as it was, with the superiority of one who knows machinery and understands its laws. Each began to have a rising respect and liking for the other.

Eugene on his part could not get over his elation about that problem.

"Some class!" he kept saying under his breath to Elsie. "Won't it be great if I'm the only one that has that problem to-morrow morning? That guy sure has a head on him. Didn't take him long to straighten the old problem out, and he saw my mistake the minute his eye lit on it. Take notice to the way he made me do the work, though? He might have been the prof the way he put me through. But I like him all right, all right! Good-night, but he must know a lot!"

Elsie sat back thoughtfully, reflecting that about now the party at her aunt's was at its height, and she was not a bit sorry she had not gone. Not for worlds would she have missed all that had happened this evening, from the hard work with her brothers up to the crowning wonderful ride in the fairy world of moonlight. The morrow might bring its cares and crosses; it doubtless would; but she would always be glad she had had this evening just as it had been. She was quite ready now to forgive the intolerant youth for his criticisms last May, since he had helped her brother out of his difficulty.

Elsie hurried away from school the next day as soon as the session was over, and took the trolley to her aunt's. She had decided to go and see whether her aunt was really ill, as Katharine had intimated, and if possible to make plain the importance of her own presence at Morningside. But, when she reached the house, she found no one at home but the maid, who said that her aunt had gone out to make calls. Elsie gave one glance about the beloved rooms where she had spent so many happy hours, and her eyes filled with tears; but she turned hastily into the little reception room to hide them from the maid, and said she would sit a few minutes at the desk there and write a note to her aunt before she left.

Then she tried to write an explanation of her inability to be absent from the home the night before but found after several attempts that it was impossible without telling too much. So she tore up her efforts, and wrote a few lines of regret that she could not come to the party and of disappointment to find them all away. She signed it, "Lovingly, Elsie," just as if nothing had happened, and went out, leaving it on the desk where she knew her aunt would be sure to find it. This was all she could do.

She looked around once more wistfully on the dear rooms, so immaculate in their quiet order, ready for the hour when the family should come home to occupy them. Yet there was not any regret in her heart for what she had done. Her own home was fully as attractive in its way, and there was a bond of the need for her that drew her now far more strongly than ever she had been bound to this home. She did not go up to the room that had been hers. Somehow she felt it was not hers any more. There had been a finality about her going from here that had made her feel she would never again enter as anything but a guest. It could not belong to her in the old sense.

She thought she was sad as she left the door; but a few minutes and she was happy again, thinking of the evening and anticipating what Eugene would have to tell about his day's experience. She was anxious to know whether anybody else had the problem and whether the professor was surprised. She thought pleasantly of the young man who had come in so informally and helped them, and of his frank, friendly way of being one with them. It did not seem possible that he was the same one who had spoken with such haughty superiority of the education of women. She felt again the frosty air on her cheek, and saw the wreaths of fog rise from the swamps as she recalled the wonderful motor trip; and then she wondered dreamily whether they would see him again often. He had said he would come and take them to ride, but so many people forget such things as soon as they are said. Well, it had been pleasant, if only for once.

Then she turned her thoughts to the dinner. She would have time if she started as soon as she got home to make a Brown Betty for dessert. Her father had said he would like one, and she knew how to make delicious ones with hard sauce. So musing, she reached her home.

The Brown Betty was all made, and Elsie was just about to sit down to a book when she happened to glance out of the window, and saw Stewart going by. She stood still a moment behind the curtain, watching him. He could not see her; and she studied his tall, well-built form, his easy stride, the way he carried his head. Her vision was arrested by the trolley stopping, and her father being assisted to get out. Was he ill? Was he—Oh! he was staggering! Staggering and shaking his fist at the conductor, who had helped him out, shouting angrily something to which the conductor replied with a contemptuous laugh. The passengers were looking at him, too, and laughing or frowning; the whole lighted car was giving its attention to their house and to her father, who was making a terrible spectacle of himself! Cameron Stewart was passing the car! He could not have helped seeing and hearing! He could not help knowing who the drunken man was or where he lived, even if he did not remember him. A great resentment filled her heart. Oh! Why did that young man always seem to be around! Always she was humiliated before him! Well, he was getting his wish! She was certainly being tried by a fiercer fire than ever burned in any kitchen range!

Her faced burned crimson. Her heart beat so wildly

that it seemed as if she could not get her breath. Her head reeled giddily. Everything in the room danced blackly before her eyes. Then she heard her father's stumbling step upon the porch; and, turning, she fled blindly up the stairs to her room, locked the door, and threw herself upon the bed, burying her face in the pillow, yet listening with her very soul for any sound of horror that might come from below.

SHE lay quite still for several seconds, her burning face hot in the pillow, her soul trying to listen for sounds from below, while the blood surged through her ears in a noisy tide that deafened her. All the time one thought was beating itself over and over in her brain, "That drunken man down there is my father!"

Suddenly she sat up with a strained, anxious look on her face, and realized that she had no time for giving way to agony. There were things to be done. There was that servant with ears and eyes probably all agog! She must somehow get her out of the house. Stealthily she opened her door and stole down the back stairs, trying in her flight to brush back her hair and erase the traces of horror from her face.

"Martha!" she said sweetly from the dusk of the stairway, "could you please run down to the store at once before it closes and get a bottle of olives?"

Martha retreated hastily from the pantry door, where she also had been listening. With knowing attitude she came toward the back stairs, her large worn-down heels and floppy shoe-soles making no sound; and, standing close to the stair door, she peered keenly into Elsie's flushed face.

"Say, now, honey, does you sho' 'nuf want dat bottle o' olives? Kase, ef you does, I think you jes' better run down yohse'f and git 'em. Dis here ain't the fust time I've seen a man come home more'n half full, and I ain't 'fraid but what I kin manage him. I wo'ked foh yoh ma oncet, an' I knows all 'bout dis business. So you jes' keep out'n it. I'll git some supper on de table, an' let him eat. Then like's not he'll go 'sleep an' you all kin come down and git yours. I'll keep it hot. Now you run 'long to yoh room, honey, and don't you fret. 'Tain't worth frettin' 'bout. My ole man used to come home dis year way many a time. There, there, honey! You run 'long, an' don't you cry." And Martha gave her an encouraging pat on the back.

Elsie stood for a moment, feeling that all the waters of trouble that the world contained were gone over her. The intolerable shame that a servant should know all about their disgrace, and speak of it as a common thing! that she should dare to open up the subject! that the circumstances were such that she had a right to offer pity and consolation! And then in her horror and dismay it came to her that this was just what Aunt Esther had meant. This was what she had sought to save her from.

With this realization came two things, a sudden pang of forgiveness and great love for the love that would have protected her; and a great, overwhelming determination to be strong and meet this terrible thing which she had no doubt she had been sent here to meet, and grapple with, and conquer, if possible.

The tears were in her eyes and rolling unheeded down her burning cheeks, but her firm little chin was lifted and set with purpose. She actually tried to smile as she stood there on the lower stair in the shadow and steadied her voice to say, "Thank you, Martha!" without choking over it.

A flush of understanding and admiration passed between the two, and there were tears on both black and white face alike. Then new horror froze Elsie's breath in her throat. Heavy footsteps were coming toward the pantry door, and they could hear muttered imprecations.

"Run upstairs, honey, girl! Let me han'le 'im!" whispered Martha, tenderly pushing Elsie away from her; but the girl stepped down beside the black woman, and stood calmly awaiting the opening of the door.

It was flung open with an angry jerk that caused it to rebound almost shut again, striking the man in the face and arousing his anger still further. This he vented on the two who stood awaiting his coming.

"Yes, here you are! Hiding away from me in my own house! Just as I expected!" he snarled, lowering his head like some wild beast and curving his hands till they made one think of claws outstretched for prey. He looked at them with his eyes narrowed into little glittering slits, all the fine manliness of his old face gone—vacant—and a beast in place of a soul. He stooped, and took a stealthy step forward as if he would spring upon them both, and began to utter a low guttural, ending in a stream of oaths.

"Run quick!" whispered Martha. "He's pretty well tanked up. He's been at it all day!"

But Elsie stepped forth from behind her protector, and in a clear voice spoke to him.

"Father! Supper is all ready. You go in and sit down in your place, and Martha and I will bring it in."

Something commanding in the clear voice held the beast in check. He straightened up, and looked at her a moment blankly as if trying to fathom her meaning. Then his eyes narrowed cunningly again, and he dropped once more into the stealthy, forward, creeping attitude:

"Oh, I know you! You want to get rid of me. Get rid of your own father! But I'll teach you to be dutiful! I'll show you that you can't run away and hide from me when I come in: You—you—you—"

A torrent of hideous language followed as the man slowly lurched forward toward the girl, who stood looking at him with frightened, fascinated eyes. Slow memories were stealing, as if a veil had been suddenly lifted that hid the past; scenes in which she had had no part, of which she had heard far echoes; times when she had been hurried out of the house or to some distant room that she might not hear or see. Was this what had made her mother's face so white and her smile so sad?

What was he going to do? Was he going to kill her, strangle her, perhaps? Why wasn't she frightened? Why didn't she run or scream? Why did she have to stand rooted to this spot on the old kitchen linoleum, with the chops burning on the gas-range and no power in her hands or feet to go and save them? And those awful words! Would she ever forget them if she lived beyond this terrible moment? They shivered through her like keen blades. He was coming nearer still. He had taken two more steps. She could smell the liquor on his breath. Would it never end, this awful waiting for him to do his worst?

Then suddenly a strong arm was flung about the man from behind; a hand shut firmly over his mouth; two other hands caught his feet, and threw him. The brothers had come and flung themselves into the scene so quietly that no one of the three had heard them.

There was a moment's struggle during which the girl closed her eyes and put her hands over her ears, waiting with trembling limbs for she knew not what. Then she was aware that the noise and struggle had ceased and Martha was drawing her down into a chair. Her brothers had carried their father up to his room. She could hear his struggles and shoutings dimly; but Martha had shut all the doors, and was smoothing her hair and saying:

"Yoh poh li'l honey chile! Don't take on so, honey! He'll sleep it all off, and he won't do nothin' to yeh. Yoh ma uset to say he wouldn't never really *do* nothin' when he was drunk'm, only jes' talk. You ain't got no call to be feared. Yoh bit brothahs 'll take good keer o' yoh, honey!"

Elsie heard Martha's tender chatter, but for some time could not take in all she was saying. She tried to smile and make the woman understand that she was grateful, but she could not speak. She was overwhelmed. It was as if she had received a revelation of the world's sin and degradation through the voice and person of her own father, and it was too much for her. She felt dazed with the horror of it all.

The boys came downstairs presently. They were stern and white. They came anxiously into the kitchen in search of her. Their eyes were flashing fire. It reminded Elsie of sparks she had once seen flying from a piece of fine steel that was held to the grindstone. She lifted a white face, and smiled a welcome to them faintly. Eugene stooped and gently kissed her on the forehead, and called her "dear" in a low tone. She was touched to tears with the suddenness and tenderness of it from this reserved brother. Jack came over, and lifted her up from the chair.

"Come on, kiddie," he said as if she were a little child, "don't take on! Why worry? You can't help it, you know. He isn't worth your tears. And anyhow he was bound to do it sooner or later, though he did hold off a long time on your account."

"He's no business to come home in that condition and frighten her!" muttered Eugene angrily. "He's no business! He owes something to Elsie at least, after she's come home to make things comfortable for us, even if he doesn't owe anything to us. Hang it all! What's the use of trying to do anything? What's the use of my trying to go to the university with a father like that? No matter what you start, you're always coming up against this."

His face was black with anger and despair. Jack lifted his own tired eyes in a white face, and looked at him despairingly.

"Well, what's the use?" he said with a kind of groan. "You can't do anything."

Then Elsie stood up and faced her brothers.

"God can!" she said solemnly. "And, yes, *we* can do something, too. We *must* do something! We *will* do something! Why, boys, we can't have him go on and live this way and then die! He mustn't die that way!"

"Die!" sneered Eugene. "It would be a godsend if he would! You don't know, Elsie. You were little. You didn't understand. We shouldn't have let you come here, I suppose. We knew it couldn't last. But he promised—-And it was so good to think of your coming."

"I'm glad I came," said Elsie. "Of course I'd come! I ought to have come before. And you're not to talk that way. Something *must* be done. If I don't understand, I'll learn. We must find a way. People *do* stop drinking. I know they do. We must *pray.*"

Elsie was not accustomed to talk religion. In her heart she had her own firm faith, but she had been brought up to keep these things to herself, and now in the stress of the moment the words seemed wrung from her like something sacred that she feared to desecrate, yet was compelled to lay hold upon.

Her brothers stared at her, and Jack laughed at her, a loud, nervous laugh.

"Pray!" he said. "I'd like to know what good you think that would do? He needs a good club, I think, coming home and getting you into this state."

"Pray!" sneered Eugene. "What good would that do? Elsie, you don't understand. He's been at it for years, and he'll keep at it to the end. There's no stopping him, and you might as well understand that now as later. You better pack up your things and go back to Aunt Esther's. This is no place for you. We ought to have known better than to let you come."

But Elsie was calm now. Somehow the mention of prayer had strengthened her. Somehow she remembered who had promised to walk beside His children in times of trouble, and a great peace descended upon her, and helped her to see things clearly.

"No, Eugene!" she said quietly. "You needn't talk of my going away. He's my father as well as yours, and I came here to stay. We'll stick together, and keep the home; and we'll work for him with all our might."

"But it isn't right to you, Elsie. You are a girl. You've had a chance to get out of this—this—this hell of a life, for that's what it's been, and you ought to stay out of it. It's no place for a girl, just as Aunt Esther said. Why, you can't have any friends coming here. You never know when he's going to come home like this and turn everything upside down. You ought to go, Elsie, you really ought."

Jack stood in the middle of the kitchen, looking miserably from one to the other of them.

"Do you want me to go, Gene?" asked Elsie, her voice trembling with appeal for her brother's love.

"No! Of course I don't want you to go, but I think you ought," responded Eugene gruffly.

"Do *you* want me to go, Jack?"

"Not on your life!" responded Jack savagely.

"Then I'm *not going!"* she answered decidedly. "Whatever comes, I'm not going. Do you understand? Please don't mention it to me again. I'm going to stay right here and help, at least until you want me to go. Now come; we're going in to eat our supper."

Martha had been going quietly back and forth carrying in the supper, and now she signified that everything was ready. Jack, big, hungry boy that he was, put his arm around Elsie's waist, and she drew her arm within Eugene's; and so the three went slowly, soberly to the table, and, sitting down, tried to be cheerful for one another's sakes. But it was hard, for upstairs an angry, muttering voice kept shouting invectives, and there was pounding on the door; and the hearts of the three children were very sore.

"Come on out and take a walk, Elsie," said Jack after supper when they had all settled down in the living-room and Eugene was at his books. The sounds of disturbance were still heard upstairs at intervals. "This gets on my nerves."

"But we mustn't leave Gene here alone, and he has to study," said Elsie, longing to go, yet held by her duty.

Eugene looked up from his books with an appreciative smile. It was so new to him to have anyone consider him that it sent a thrill through him every time.

"I don't mind, really, kid," he said tenderly. "I'm used to it, you know; and, besides, this book is awfully interesting. I'll just stay here and keep at it. I've got to write a review of it yet to-night, you know, or I'd go too."

So they slipped away in the moonlight, brother and sister, and walked about the streets of Morningside for an hour or more, passing houses lit up where people sat happily around tables reading and talking; looking in wistfully and wondering whether these too had hidden sorrows that might break out at any time and spoil the beauty and the comfort of the home. Jack opened his heart to his sister, revealing many of his boyish hopes and fears, how he used to dread to go into the house at night, because always his mother's coffin seemed to be there in the parlor when he first entered, and how Elsie's coming had dispelled the dreadful vision of that white, sad face. He told her how he used to lie and cry himself to sleep nights when his father was drunk, and wish and pray that he might die before morning; and how it used to hurt him to know that every one knew their shame. He let her know that he had felt that God was against them all for his father's sin, and he had often felt how useless it was to try to do anything right because there was God hating him for something he couldn't help.

He didn't say all these things in just this way; he merely revealed them by his words, till all the cry and longing of his heart had been spoken out. Elsie forgot her own shame and sorrow in the pitiful picture of this lonely young life, and reached her hand into Jack's overcoat pocket after his big hand, nestling in it comfortingly.

"But God does care, dear. I know he does. Haven't things been a little better lately?" She asked it wistfully.

He grasped the little hand strongly in his own.

"You mean since you came? You bet they have! It hasn't been the same house. It's like heaven. It's something like living now. It's been wonderful. I don't see why you did it, such a mess as things were here, and you had everything fine at Aunt Esther's."

"I think God sent me," she said thoughtfully. "I didn't really want to come at all at first. I was interested in things in the city, and I had got weaned away from here.

It was all wrong. I ought never to have gone away at all, I guess, or at least only for a little while till I got old enough to help make a home and know how to do things right. But I ought never to have been satisfied to stay there and live my life out without you. And yet I was. But, when I came out here that first day that I straightened things up a little, I felt something drawing me that I could not understand. And now I know that it must have been God telling me I was living where I did not belong, and I ought to get back to my place, and love it, and make it beautiful. It was because God loved you, Jack, that He made things different for us all."

"It doesn't look much as if He loved you, bringing you into this," murmured the brother with drawn brows. "I thought for a while that maybe Father was going to be different, now that you had come; but it didn't last; and you oughtn't to have to bear it."

"Why not? Hard things make one grow strong. It isn't a sign that God doesn't love you just because He lets you get some hard knocks. You wouldn't think a boy would be much account, would you, if he was brought up without hard knocks, just everything made easy for him?"

So they walked about the town and talked until both felt strengthened for the fight they saw before them.

It was all quiet at the house when they returned, and Eugene was just finishing his book-review. When it was done and the paper folded, Elsie shyly took a hand of each brother, and drew them over toward the couch.

Wonderingly they followed her, and then she paused beside the couch and looked up at them bravely.

"Will you kneel down with me?" she whispered wistfully.

Embarrassed, yet not liking to refuse, the two big fellows knelt one on each side of her, their arms protectingly thrown about her; and kneeling so, with the flicker of the firelight upon them and the silent tragedy in the room above them, Elsie breathed her first audible prayer. It was a stumbling, halting, childlike petition; but it came from a heart full of longing and sorrow. It was very brief, only two or three sentences; but, simple as it was, it must have reached the Throne. The two big fellows found tears upon their cheeks, and they bowed their heads the lower, and had to struggle to keep back their own strong feelings. After the "Amen" they continued to kneel in silence for a minute or two; and, when they rose, they each in turn bent over their sister and kissed her good-night; but they had no language but their tears to show her how they appreciated her presence and her fine, sweet personality.

SEVERAL times that evening and far into the night Cameron Stewart walked by the house in the stillness of the shadows, and kept watch with aching heart. He watched the lights go out one by one and quiet settle on the house; and again and yet again he walked by, that he might make sure that all was well. As he walked, he fought out something in his own heart, and tried to understand himself.

Was it just sympathy that made him feel so keenly for this lovely girl? She was almost a stranger to him; yet he felt so strangely drawn to her. Something recoiled within him at thought of her belonging to the man who had reeled off the trolley crying out invectives to the world. It seemed a hard thing that a man had a right to shame his own child in this way. When he thought of the lovely face of that girl as it must have looked when she saw her father, his very soul boiled within him with rage; and yet there was with it mingled a kind of pity for the poor creature who had allowed himself to become a slave to a habit that crazed him and unmanned him. It was of no use to wonder where the poor fellow got the liquor, of course as long as respectable people insisted upon having it, there would always be ways for tempted men to get it. The pity of it was that a girl like Elsie Hathaway had to be hurt by it. Such a bud of a girl, scarcely more than a child, and such a fine, sweet, brilliant girl too! If only he could do something to lift this sorrow from her life!

The next afternoon as he drove his car down one of the principal city streets, he saw Mr. Hathaway ambling slowly, aimlessly toward him with uncertain gait. A glance made it plain that he was still under the influence of liquor, though by no means in the critical condition in which he had been the evening before.

The truth was he had cunningly evaded Jack's vigilance and made his way to the river, always his ultimate destination when despair overtook him and his own selfishness was revealed to him.

How long he had stood shivering beside the murky water, looking down and thinking how it would be to lie beneath it with the boats stealing over his upturned face, and his eyes open always to the accusing heavens, he did not know. The usual climax was reached in the course of time, and an inextinguishable thirst clamored to be satisfied.

He turned his footsteps away from the dramatic death he had never really meant to attempt, and hurried down into the city. He threaded his way this way and that through the streets, and suddenly there was a great car stopping beside the curb and a man leaning out to speak to him. He stopped, and tried to understand with his poor, bewildered brain.

"Won't you get in and ride with me, Mr. Hathaway?"

Was it possible the man was asking him, *him?*

He climbed unsteadily into the back seat, and allowed the stranger to wrap him up warmly. Then they whirled off through the streets, threading their way through the traffic, and finally getting out into the wide open thoroughfare. He soon fell into a profound sleep.

For hours they flew over the road. Just as the dusk was dropping down about them they halted at a little inn in a quiet country town.

Mr. Hathaway opened his eyes, and looked about in a dazed way. He wondered who the man was who was talking to him; but he got out and followed in where the lights shone and where little round tables were covered with white cloths.

Food was being brought. There was hot oyster broth! It made him giddy to smell it. It tasted good, and he ate it greedily. It seemed to steady his nerves and send a tingle of life to his trembling fingers again. It gave him courage. There was a smell of coffee in the air. Yes, they were bringing coffee, smoking hot, and beefsteak, and other things. He ate and drank, and grew saner with every mouthful. About eight o'clock the telephone bell rang in Morningside and Elsie answered it.

"That you, Elsie? Well, this is Dad. Yes, I'm all right. Yes, I'm taking a little automobile trip with a friend, and I'll be home before midnight. Don't sit up, and don't you worry. Understand? I'm *all right!*"

Shortly before midnight as softly as a car can go they slid up to the curb in front of the house, and Mr. Hathaway got out.

But, quiet as they had been, Elsie was on the alert, and in her pink and silver robings was standing behind her rose curtains, peering out.

The car had stopped just behind the big lilac bush, so that she could not see who was driving it; but she heard a low voice say:

"You usually go in town on the trolley, don't you? Well, how about going with me to-morrow morning? I shall be going quite early. You have to be at your office at eight o'clock? Well, I'll be at this corner at half past seven. That will give us plenty of time. Good-night."

The car slid away into the shadows again, and Mr. Hathaway came steadily up the front walk with a self-respecting gait. Elsie slipped into bed with relief, and wondered what there was about the voice of the man that sounded so familiar.

For three days Cameron Stewart had been taking Mr. Hathaway into town in the morning and bringing him out at night in his car, always managing to do it so unobservedly that as yet none of the family had found out. The third day, however, Jack happened to be home a little earlier than usual, and was standing at the front window when the car drew up to the curb behind the lilac bush and then whizzed silently away in the dusk. When his father came in, he asked:

"Who's your friend, Dad? Some class to you arriving in a big six car like that."

"It's not the first time," grinned his father proudly. "Been going and coming for several days like that. Some car, isn't it?"

"Yes, whose is it?"

"Why, his name is Stewart. He picked me up on Chestnut Street a few days ago, and since then we've been real chummy. He's a nice, likely fellow. You ought to hear him talk."

"Stewart! You don't mean it! Well, he's some peach, he is! I wonder what he does it for."

"Oh, just to be sociable, I guess. Says he's lonesome going and coming alone all the time."

Elsie hovering in the hall fearfully, as she always did now when her father came home, heard the whole conversation, and stood looking out of the window thinking. It had been his voice, then, she had heard in the moonlight that night! She echoed Jack's question in her heart, while her eyes grew strangely soft as she stared into the dusk.

The days that followed were happy ones, although they were fraught with a certain degree of nervous anxiety. Each night the three children watched their father's home-coming with tense, strained nerves, and relaxed into comforted sighs of relief when they saw him come steadily up the walk. Each morning his daughter's heart was filled with prayer as she saw him go forth, always sending up a thankful song when she saw him climb into an automobile instead of a car in the dim morning light; and this happened as often as two or three times a week.

Cameron Stewart was not forcing himself upon them. He did not come in to call for a whole week after the evening when Mr. Hathaway had come home under the influence of liquor. He wanted to let the circumstance be forgotten, so that his presence might not embarrass them. But when he came, Elsie let him know by the look in her eyes and the way in which she welcomed him that she was grateful to him. Nothing was said, of course; but he understood that she understood, and he was fully repaid for the small sacrifice he had made to help the old man past the hour of temptation and establish him in safe habits again.

It was almost pitiful, the way Mr. Hathaway came forward to welcome Cameron Stewart. A little of his old brightness and courtesy seemed to have returned to him while the visitor was there. He told several witty stories, and entered into the conversation with a zest that made his own boys look at him with wonder. But Elsie sat quiet for the most part, watching the visitor, and letting the others do the talking.

At last Stewart turned to her.

"Now, you'll play for us, won't you?" he said with

that bright smile that always won the hearts of people. And Elsie arose and went to the piano. There were things she wanted to say to this guest that she could not put into words—questions she would ask and gratitude she would speak. She might not let him know by her lips how she felt about it all, but she could tell him with the music. Perchance he would understand.

So she played for him alone, forgetting the others, forgetting even that he might be a musician himself, or at least a musical critic, and therefore able to see mistakes and flaws in her technique. She was not thinking of herself. She was playing with her heart, making the phrases of the old composers speak things she could not put into words, ask questions she dared not frame, give thanks for intangible help that lay all unrecognized in any other way between them.

Her father sat there happily watching, thinking how she resembled her mother, proud that the stranger liked her playing. He was not thinking much about the music himself. The brothers, with their books around the big table, looked up and listened now and then when some melody pleased them. They were conscious that it was being well done. They did not care greatly for such music themselves. They heard the pleasant sound of it, and saw the interest in the visitor's face. He gave the deference due to their sister. They were content. The music meant nothing extraordinary to them. It was only to the young man that it spoke and revealed the hidden beauties of the girl's soul, her fears and hopes, and wistful thanks, perhaps.

The fire burned low, and the soft lamplight fell over the girl as she played, making a pretty picture. The young man sat in his shadowed corner, and watched her.

It was a wonderful time to both of them and the beginning of a great understanding between them.

Before he went home he talked over another problem with Eugene, gave Jack an amusing account of his visit to Stratford on Avon apropos of the Shakespeare play Jack was reading with a view to examination, and sang college songs with the three for an hour; but Elsie's music had been the heart of the evening to him.

It was an interesting coincidence that Cameron Stewart's car was gliding slowly by the schoolhouse the next afternoon just as Elsie came out of the door to catch her car. Probably nobody in the street had noticed that he had gone by three times before that afternoon; but this time he drew up to the curb, and what more natural than that he should ask Elsie whether she was going out to Morningside and would ride with him?

That ride meant a great deal to Elsie. She had been out in as beautiful cars before, and often with delightful young men who were, as her cousins used to say, "crazy about her"; but she had never taken such a ride as that. When she came to think about it and ask herself why she enjoyed it so much, she could not explain it to herself. Halsey Kennedy could talk, not so well perhaps, but interestingly. It was not the conversation, though that had been delightful, all about books and music and art, and what Elsie called "real things." But it was not the conversation. The day was perfect as winter days can be, cold and bracing, but not too sharp. Still, there had been perfect days before. The car was luxury itself, and its driver was fully its master; but luxurious cars and easy drivers were not hard to find. No, it was something deeper and subtler than that. It was a sympathy between them, a kind of understanding even before a word was spoken, that made the day and themselves in tune with one another, and made the miles to Morningside, though they went by the longest possible route, fly by in a trice.

It was on that ride that Stewart mentioned that he had tickets for the Boston Symphony concert the next week, with Paderewski as soloist, and asked her whether she would like to go.

She flashed a smile full of the light of joy up to him; and then her face grew sober, and she was still for a minute without making him any answer. At last she said, very low and sadly:

"Mr. Stewart, you are a stranger in Morningside. Do you know—about—my father?"

She lifted her brave eyes to his face, and drew herself up proudly. She was almost sure he knew; yet she would take no chances.

He looked down into her true, loyal eyes; and a great wave of admiration passed over him. He could not keep it out of his eyes, though he controlled his voice to answer gently, meaningfully.

"Yes, I know."

And there was no pity in his voice, only sympathy, kind and deep and understanding. Not even a shred of patronage or of lack of respect for her because of what he knew. His eyes answered every challenge in her own until all were satisfied. Then a great content came into hers, with a light as if some one had lit them, and she said with a little happy ring to her voice:

"Than I shall be very glad to go. I couldn't go anywhere with anyone unless he perfectly understood."

He smiled.

"Did I look like that kind of a cad?"

She laughed merrily as if a great load had suddenly rolled away from her.

"No, you didn't. That was why I had to protect you!" she said.

The next Monday night they went to the concert, Elsie happy in the fact that Eugene had taken Jack to some doings at his frat house, and her father had to stay in town to do some night work in connection with a special invoice his firm was making; so no one would miss her.

The Academy of Music was full that night in honor of the great soloist and beloved orchestra.

High up in the family circle Katharine and Bettina sat with their father and mother, discontentedly watching the favored people in the balcony boxes.

Katharine sat with the opera-glasses raised to her eyes, idly watching the people below her as they came in and settled to their places.

Suddenly she pressed the glasses into Bettina's hand.

"Look! Look quick! There goes Elsie! Down in the balcony box to the left, the third seat from the centre, the best seat in the house. See! There! They're sitting down. Don't you see him taking off her cloak, Elsie's old gray one with the gray fur. Do you see her?"

"Yes, I see her. She's got an awfully good-looking man with her! He must have some money to get seats down there. Look at the roses she's wearing. Aren't they superb? How in the world did she meet a man like that out in Morningside?"

"Oh, you can't tell anything by his looks!" sneered her sister. "He may be some poor clerk whose firm has given him some tickets they couldn't use, and he's making a big splurge for once. Let me look again. It surely is Elsie, isn't it?"

"Sure! Don't you recognize the little blue velvet hat with the silver brim? Look, Mother! There's Elsie down in a balcony box. And with the most stunning-looking man! See, Katharine, he's got a fur-lined overcoat. No mere clerk would have a fur-lined overcoat."

"You can't tell," sneered Katharine. "He may put his whole salary on his back."

But Uncle James had reached over and secured the opera-glasses and was looking now with all his might.

"H'm!" he said significantly when he had got a good look, "I should say she had got a man this time! A real man. Do you know who that is down there with your cousin, Katharine?"

"No. Do you know him, Father?"

"Well, I rather guess I do. It's Cameron Stewart. About the biggest thing in the way of a rising young engineer this city can produce. He's had all sorts of flattering offers, and they say he can get any salary, almost, that he demands. He's done something or other—made some big discovery or invention—that changes the situation in electrical engineering considerably, and every big corporation in the city is after him. Sure, he wears fur-lined overcoats! He can have a new one for every style of weather that's made if he wants to."

"And you say you know him, Father?"

"Yes, I know him quite well. We've drawn up the contracts for several of his big operations, and I've arranged everything with him personally myself."

"Why didn't you ever bring him out to see us, papa?" asked Bettina, aggrieved.

"Why didn't I bring the moon home to dinner?" answered her father with a laugh. "Well, because Stewart is very exclusive. It isn't an easy thing to bring a man like that home. They say he's quite reserved, and doesn't go out much. He's rather a big person to ask home to dinner, Betty, dear. I shouldn't have felt exactly comfortable doing it. For a young man he's very distant and dignified. He doesn't strike me as the kind of man you ask offhand to come home with you. It really never occurred to me."

"How in the world could Elsie ever meet a man like

that?" exclaimed her aunt indignantly, as if Elsie had no right to meet respectable people without her assistance.

Then the music began in a crashing burst of jubilation, and the aunt and cousins were obliged to confine their speculations to the opera-glasses and their own cogitations, watching jealously every time Stewart leaned over to speak to Elsie or hand her the programme, or help adjust her cloak that was slipping from the back of her chair.

Elsie, meantime, was supremely unconscious of the jealous eyes upon her, and sat in a dream of bliss. She had been hungry for some music; for in spite of her consuming interest in the things of her new-old home, and her desire to help on with her brother's studies, she had sighed in secret now and then for some of the things she had been used to in the city. And the programme before her was one of unusual interest. Moreover, the man beside her was in perfect sympathy with her mood; he loved music—loved best the kind of music she had loved, for they had talked about it on the way down—and was watching her enjoyment and answering her every appreciative glance with another fully as appreciative. Could music be heard under happier circumstances?

Then there were the flowers she wore, lovely, delicate buds of rosy golden color, perfumed like a baby's breath; and there she was sitting in the very best place in the whole Academy, where she had seldom been before, with an escort all might see to be a peer among men. What more could mortal girl desire in the way of a setting for a wonderful concert?

It was no wonder that she forgot to look up to the family circle and wonder whether any of her aunt's family were present, forgot them entirely, although just before she started from Morningside her heart had been a little sore at the thought that they had not written nor paid any attention yet to all her advances.

Katharine and Bettina got very little cultural benefit from the concert that night. Their eyes and their thoughts were down in that balcony box watching Elsie; and, when they saw the young man flash a smile of appreciation at their cousin, and her answering smile of understanding, they began to conclude that their cousin had known this man a long time and had kept them in ignorance of it—wanted to keep him all for herself, perhaps—was their unworthy thought. For, when suspicion once creeps into a heart, even of one who loves, there is no telling where it may stop.

"I wonder if *that's* what took her out to Morningside," said Katharine at the close of the concert as she stood watching the efficient way in which Stewart helped Elsie with her coat. "Betty, he certainly is stunning, isn't he? I think I'll go out and see Elsie on Saturday and find out about this."

KATHARINE was as good as her word. She went to Morningside on Saturday, but she went like an army with banners. She had no intention of meeting the enemy alone on alien ground. She felt that if she went with the proper people Elsie would not dare to turn her down for anything. So she took Halsey Kennedy into her plan, and with her sister and two other young men they started early Saturday afternoon in Kennedy's big touring car for Morningside. The plan was to take Elsie with them and make an afternoon of it, winding up at the city home for dinner and an evening entertainment, and if possible, keeping Elsie with them over Sunday. Katharine felt it was high time that Elsie was rescued and brought back to her proper element. She thought the alienation had gone on fully long enough, especially since Elsie seemed to have annexed an altogether desirable young man who would be a great addition to their circle. There was no reason whatever why Elsie shouldn't come back to the city to live again. If there were things that needed to be done out at Morningside, they could all help her do them, and Papa would of course give them money to hire some one to see to things at Morningside, if there were no other way. Anyway, Elsie must come back. That was settled.

But when they arrived at Morningside, Martha informed them: "Miss Elsie done gone out in de machine wid a young man, an' she won't be home till long 'bout five o'clock."

Katharine, greatly vexed, pondered on what she should do; for of course the whole plan was upset now, and their ride must be carried out without Elsie. Halsey Kennedy would have an all-day grouch because she hadn't telephoned that they were coming, and everything would be disagreeable. What could she do?

But Katharine was a young woman of resources, and it did not take her long to think of a way out of it.

To her relief she spied a telephone in the hall. Somebody must be secured to take the ride with Halsey Kennedy, or he would spoil the whole plan. She would telephone to Rose Maddern, who lived at Lynwoode, four or five miles farther on, and get her to take the afternoon ride with them. Halsey liked Rose, and would get on well with her on the front seat. Then they could return about five o'clock, leave Rose at her home, and pick up Elsie. She would write a note and leave it for Elsie, telling her to be ready, so they would not be delayed on the way back. Halsey would be satisfied if Elsie returned with them.

So she stepped inside the hall, and asked Martha for a pencil.

"Jes' go into the livin'-room, an' set down to Miss Elsie's desk" said Martha, grandly waving the guest inside.

In amazement Katharine looked about her at the pleasant room with its altogether delightful furnishings, the open fire burning sleepily away in the fireplace, the books and magazines, and, above all, the flowers. A great mass of chrysanthemums on the mantel, repeated in the mirror; a tall glass vase on the piano, holding pink and white carnations filling the room with their spicy breath; and on the table a bunch of lovely little yellow rosebuds like the ones Elsie had worn at the concert. Of all things! Who keeps her in flowers this way? It must be serious if all these things come from one person.

She dropped down at the desk, a lovely little mahogany affair, well appointed and standing open for the convenience of anyone. Nothing could have been more cozy and delightful than the whole charming room. Katharine could scarcely write, so filled with amazement she was.

She left her note in Martha's hands with many injunctions to have her mistress ready for their return. She telephoned to Rose Maddern, and found her delighted to go motoring with them, and then went out to the waiting company.

Halsey Kennedy was only half appeased with Rose Maddern for company. He kept half a grouch during the entire afternoon. On the whole, Katharine did not enjoy her ride so much as she had expected to do. She kept puzzling over those flowers and the general air of prosperity that had reigned in that living-room. Somehow she did not feel just so sure that her cousin would be eager to come back to the city to live now that she had seen that pleasant room. She was not altogether sure, even, that her mandates for that evening would be obeyed. She kept casting uneasy glances at Halsey Kennedy, and inquiring what time it was, until her companion told her she was a regular crab.

When they returned to Morningside, it was fully half-past five, and Katharine was keyed up tensely, resolved to resort to any lengths rather than fail of bringing

Elsie back to the city with her. She could hardly wait for the car-door to be opened that she might fly to the house and insist that her cousin hurry out.

But Elsie forstalled her plans by suddenly rushing out of the house to greet them and insisting that they all get out and come in if only for a few minutes. She looked so pretty with her cheeks all glowing from her recent ride that everyone obeyed her forthwith in spite of Katharine's protest that they would need to hurry right home because Mamma would expect them and have dinner all ready.

Elsie had them all into the living-room eagerly, joyously, and was pulling off motor-veils and cloaks before they could stop her.

"Yes, you must," she declared laughingly. "I've got hot chocolate with whipped cream all ready for you. It will warm you up for the ride. See! Here it comes. It won't delay you a minute."

Martha entered with a tray bearing little cups with the steaming chocolate, a great bowl of whipped cream, a plate of tiny sandwiches, another of little cakes; and the company surrendered. Somehow there was something about Elsie that commanded the whole situation and threw out Katharine's calculations entirely. She moved about among them, offering more cream and cakes, and saying all the little pleasant, winning things that Elsie had always known how to say, and Katharine sat and stared at her, wondering how it could be possible that Elsie had seemed to take her surroundings with her into the country, and not to be at all upset by having all these gay young people coming out to search for her in her seclusion. In fact, half of Katharine's plans were spoiled by having the house look so different from the way it had in the days when she used to come out to see her cousins years ago. Katharine had expected the contrast to be greater, and had thought that from very shame Elsie would want to come with them to keep the others from finding out how plain and shabby her present home was.

But on the contrary Elsie was quite eager to show them all about, and kept saying how delightful it was to have them come to her. When the chocolate and cakes were finished and Katharine began to clamor for her cousin to get her hat and cloak and come on, Elsie quietly drew her cousins up into her room on the pretence of smoothing their hair; and on the way up she began to explain.

"Katharine, I'm so sorry I have another engagement to-night—," she began.

"Engagement! Oh, bother the engagement! You've got to break it and go with us. That's what we brought the boys along for, to take you by force if you wouldn't go any other way. You've simply *got* to come, or Halsey Kennedy will eat us all up on the way home. He had the worst kind of a grouch all the afternoon because I hadn't telephoned you we were coming. You can't get out of it this time!

Then she suddenly stopped in the door of the room, and stared around, speechless. To find a room like this, a lady's bower, in the old house that she remembered as gloomy and poverty-stricken was too astonishing.

But Bettina cried out:

"O Elsie! What a darling room! Who did it? Not you. It must have cost a lot of money! That sweet little desk, and that love of a bed and bureau! Just look at the walls, Katharine. Aren't they a dream? And isn't that a stunning rug? Who did it? Tell me quick! And that single rose in a cut-glass vase! Who sends you all the flowers anyway? 'Fess up quick! You can't fool us any longer. There's some man out here, or you never would have come. We saw you Monday night at the concert. Come, tell us who supplies the flowers."

Elsie smiled sweetly, and answered composedly:

"Why, my brothers had the room done over when I came, and Jack brought me the rose last night. He almost never fails to bring me some kind of a flower once or twice a week. Eugene brought home the carnations yesterday afternoon, and the chrysanthemums came from a neighbor's. She has a lot of them both indoors and out. The outside kind are all gone now, of course; but she's wild over them, and raises them just for the fun of watching them grow."

"And those perfectly nifty yellow buds downstairs?" demanded Katharine keenly. "You haven't accounted for those."

Elsie's cheeks were a shade rosier, perhaps, but she answered quietly enough:

"Mr. Stewart brought those over when he came to take me out in his car this afternoon."

"Yes, I told you so! I knew some man brought you out here!" declared Bettina teasingly.

"Betty, dear, I came out here because I thought I ought to. Father and the boys needed me. Mother would have wanted me to. You don't understand how things were and how much they needed a woman who loved them to make a real home for them."

Katharine spoke up sharply.

"Now, Elsie, you needn't get sentimental about them. You know perfectly well you were contented enough for five years without scarcely seeing them. You couldn't have been pining with love for brothers and a father who never came near you."

Elsie's cheeks glowed; but a softness came into her eyes and voice, and she answered quietly:

"Yes, I know, Katharine. I wasn't very loving, and I

didn't come out here in the first place because I loved them. I came because I saw I was needed and nobody else could possibly take my place. Then when I got here and found how they loved me, the love came. Why, Katharine, look around! See this room. My brothers did all this for me before I came. They took their own money and bought this furniture, and had this room papered and fixed up. There was a rose in that vase when I came. They hung those pictures, and made everything as nice as they knew how. Do you think I wouldn't love them after that? There hasn't been a day since I've been home that this little vase has been empty of some kind of flower, and they watch me at every turn to see whether there is anything they can do for me."

"Well, they ought to!" snapped Katharine to hide her emotion. "Look at what you gave up for them. Look how you are educated while they have been contented—"

But a shout from downstairs broke in upon her remarks.

"Elsie! Where are you? I've only a minute to catch the return car! Do you know where I put that theme I wrote last night?"

It was Eugene's voice. He had evidently just burst into the front door, and had not yet realized the presence of strangers in the house. Elsie was at the head of the stairs instantly.

"Yes, Gene, I put the theme in the upper drawer of my desk. Wait, I'll get it for you."

"No, don't bother to come down. I'll get it. I brought out the tickets. I'll lay them on your desk. Tell Jack there's enough for him to take that girl along."

Elsie, followed by her curious cousins, hurried downstairs, and found Eugene standing bewildered in the doorway of the living-room.

"Eugene has to catch that car that's coming; so please excuse us," said Elsie to her guests.

Eugene came forward with unconscious ease, grasped the hand of each guest in turn quickly, and murmured a smiling, "Awfully sorry I can't stay to get acquainted; but the team's called early to-night, and I can't miss this car."

He grasped the paper Elsie handed him, gave her the tickets, told her to be sure to come to the Franklin Street entrance and not to be late, and sped away just in time to whirl himself upon the tail end of the trolley as it passed the house.

Elsie, as she turned to glance at her cousins on the stairs, almost broke down laughing, they looked so astonished and bewildered.

"Eugene is on the varsity basket-ball team, and there is a game with Princeton to-night, you know," she explained as the two young men turned away from the window where they had watched to see whether Eugene caught the car.

"I didn't know you had a brother in the university," exclaimed Halsey Kennedy with a new note of respect in his voice, while Katharine and Bettina grasped the stair-railing and looked at each other in wonder, telegraphing each to the other not to let the men know that they had been unaware of their cousin's progress.

"He entered this fall," said Elsie coolly. "Of course it's unusual for a freshman to get on the varsity team; but Tod Hopkins, the captain, was an old chum of Eugene's in the high school, and knew what a good player he was. I suspect that had something to do with it."

"Tod Hopkins!" gasped Katharine. "Do you know Tod Hopkins?"

"Not yet," smiled Elsie. "But he's coming home to dinner with Gene next Thursday, and I expect to know him then. He's been fine to Gene, and he's already got

Jack 'lined up,' as he calls it, for next year. Jack is just crazy about Tod Hopkins."

"Does Jack go to the university too?" burst forth Bettina, unmindful of her sister's warning nudge.

"He expects to enter next fall," said Elsie sweetly. "He's studying hard, and is to take his entrance examinations in the spring."

"I think we had better be going," said Katharine haughtily. Things were getting on her nerves. "Mamma will be worried about us, and the dinner will be spoiled. Come, Elsie, aren't you going with us?"

"I'm sorry, Katharine, but you know I couldn't miss seeing Gene play his first game with Princeton. Besides Mr. Stewart and Miss Garner are going with us. It would be impossible, you know. I expect Jack in any minute."

And with that word Jack rushed in, handsome, sparkling, his dark hair tossed from the old cap he yanked off as he came in, his face eager and flushed, his eyes full of anticipation. He looked a splendid picture of perfect young manhood.

"Hello, Elsie. Did the tickets come? I asked her, anyway, O—!" and then he spied the guests, and stopped abashed.

But nothing could abash Jack for more than a second. He came forward easily the next instant.

"Why, hello, Katharine! Bettina! Awfully glad to see you! It's ages since you were out here."

He took his introductions to the two young men with nonchalance also, and Elsie watched him with pleased eyes. Certainly there was nothing about either of her brothers of which to be ashamed.

Bettina and Katharine perceived that their cousin was good to look upon. In fact, it suddenly dawned upon them that they had been letting two perfectly good young men cousins, who would have made altogether interesting and ornamental escorts, stay in the background too long. They hurried down the last three stairs, and then proceeded to make up for lost time. Bettina especially was much taken with Jack, and began one of her pretty little flirtations.

"You never come down to see us anymore," she pouted charmingly.

Jack looked at her in wonder, and grinned wisely. Something had changed the social atmosphere tremendously within the last few days. He wondered what it was. He looked at Elsie amusedly, and saw how pleased she was; wherefore, he refrained from several telling cuts wherewith he was about to chastise Bettina for her long neglect of them all, and with the most delightful effrontery proceeded to do what he called "kid" her. This Bettina liked.

"Mamma is going to have you all down to dinner soon," she ventured giving an audacious glance at Katharine; then a sudden silence settled on them all for an instant, and Elsie heard footsteps coming up the walk. They stumbled on the upper step and came on hurriedly, as one out of breath. For an instant Elsie's heart stopped beating, and she grew white to the lips. Could it be that her father had been drinking again? Was he coming in among them all to disgrace them? She took a quick step toward the door, and at the same moment Jack slid before her, his lips set firmly. If there was anything the matter with their father, he did not intend that their guests should know it.

But the door swung open hastily, and Mr. Hathaway, much excited, burst into the hall. Bettina and Katharine stood close by the living-room door, but he did not notice them. He spoke to Elsie.

"Say, Elsie, has my laundry come home yet? Jack's telephoned me he has a ticket for me to go to the game in town this evening, and I ought to catch that half past six train. He says the car will be too late. I missed my usual car, and I'm late. I guess I'll have to hustle. I shouldn't like to miss seeing Gene play."

Elsie drew a long breath of relief, and smiled. His voice was clear and eager, and the pleasure of a child was in his face. There was no smell of liquor on his breath.

"Oh, that's all right, Father; we have plenty of time. Mr. Stewart is going to take us all in his car. He left word that you were to go with us. Come in and see who is here."

"Oh!" said Mr. Hathaway, straightening up and looking pleased, "in Mr. Stewart's car? That's nice. Then we won't have to hurry. Why, Betty! That you! And Katharine! Well, this is great. I've scarcely seen you since you were little girls. Got to be young ladies now, haven't you? Well, I'm real glad to see you. Elsie here gets lonesome, I guess, sometimes with nothing but men around. Why don't you come real often?"

He greeted the strangers half shyly and then, abashed, retired to a shadowed corner of the room, the light of eagerness suddenly dying out of his eyes. In the presence of men he always wore that look of apology.

Nevertheless, Katharine, studying him carefully, saw that he had an air of rejuvenation about him, that his eyes were brighter, his whole attitude more self-respecting than she remembered him ever to have had before. He was not bad looking. In fact, he was rather a distinguished looking old man, if he only wouldn't slink into the corner so and act as if he didn't want to be seen. Nevertheless, she could see that he adored Elsie, and she turned and looked curiously at her cousin as if there, too, she saw signs of things she had never suspected in her character before. Why had Elsie been willing to leave their home and come out here? It was perfectly marvelous what Elsie had accomplished in so short a time; but why, WHY, did anybody want to do hard things like that, that they didn't have to do? She couldn't understand it. Her own nature was ease-loving, fun-loving, selfishly inclined. Suddenly she realized that it was time they were going. If Elsie was really not going home with them, they had better cut the agony short. Halsey Kennedy would have an unremovable grouch, of course. One could see it coming on now. His eyebrows were drawn down, and his lips stuck out twice their usual thickness. He had already realized that Elsie was hopelessly out of the evening plans, and felt himself tricked into a most dull and uninteresting afternoon with no compensations for the evening. He felt it his immediate duty to get even with Katharine by not speaking to her all the way into the city.

So Katharine, crestfallen, filled with varying emotions, retired from the field of defeat. But, as she was going out the door, she showed her mettle and the glorious way in which she could surrender by turning toward her cousins with a ravishing smile, which included the poor old uncle in the background, and saying:

"Mamma is going to want you all to come to dinner very soon, you know, and you really must find a date when everyone of you can come."

Then the invading party crowded morosely into their car and departed.

"Gee whillikins!" ejaculated Jack as he closed the door behind them. "Now *what* do you suppose she did that for?"

"Why, I guess she is just coming to herself, Jack, dear," mused Elsie with a smile. "You know really Katharine is all right if she just understands. She is beginning to understand."

"I should think it was about time!" growled Jack to

his necktie as he took the stairs at a stride, and proceeded to make a rapid toilet for the basket-ball game.

He was very much pleased that Elsie had suggested his taking Ruby Garner with them. Ruby was a witch of a girl with yellow hair and brown eyes and the cherriest cheeks and lips. All the boys in high school were crazy about her. She had dimples and the most charming little smile. She had been in the grammar school when Jack stopped going to the high school. He hadn't seen her often since, but they were pretty good friends. She told him her troubles sometimes. Her mother had died a year ago, and her father was away a great deal. Jack was wonderfully pleased that she admired Elsie. He thought she needed a girl friend. He had rather hazy ideas of proprieties himself, but he liked to think of Ruby as being guarded by wise friends. He hadn't an idea that Elsie was getting acquainted with Ruby for his sake.

He wasn't quite sure how Elsie found out that he rather liked Ruby. He was positive he hadn't told her himself. It was awfully decent of Stewart to send word he might bring a girl along, and to take Father too. Poor Dad! He didn't have many pleasures. How kiddish he acted about going! People didn't grow old, even if they had lived a long time. He wondered whether he ever should. He wondered whether next year, when he got into the university, they would all go down to see him play basket-ball some night—and bring Ruby!

He lifted his chin, and drew the knot of his tie closer, smiling at himself in the glass, then, whirling into his coat, he went whistling down to the dinner-table to snatch a bite before the car came.

On the whole, Elsie was quite content as she got into the front seat with Stewart and had the luxurious fur robes tucked about her. The pretty girl whom they picked up at the third corner looked just a mischievous, sweet child, and not at all dangerous for Jack as a friend. Elsie felt she could like her at once, and resolved to make friends with her. It was not nearly so bad as if Jack had taken a notion to some bold, loud girl with pencilled eyebrows and befloured countenance. Little Ruby was quite awed and childlike in the presence of the sister and the father and this elegant young man who touched his hat as if she were a queen, and helped to tuck the robes about her when she settled down into the back seat beside Jack. She was filled with delight over the prospect of the ride in such a car and the game she was to attend. Her eyes sparkled, and her dimples came and went bewitchingly. Her voice was low and sweet when she answered shyly the few questions they put to her now and then. Elsie felt that her presence was not going to spoil the little party at all.

With her mind at ease about Jack and her father, with pleasant anticipations of the game and Gene's part in it, with the gloomy background of her troubles with her cousins pleasantly removed, Elsie was free to enjoy the companionship of Stewart, and the swift, beautiful ride to the university. And all the way her heart kept singing. She was becoming convinced that, when one was faithfully going according to one's conscience, sooner or later the way would be opened and the clouds break.

IT WAS a lovely day, one of those when the air is filled with new perfume, and the buzz of contented bees who find no trouble in filling their honey storehouses. Even the sparrows of the city were glad, and gave a festive air to the close-growing-ivy-covered walls of the school buildings. Cameron Stewart as he stopped his automobile in front of the stone steps of the Library building where Professor Bowen was awaiting him, felt like a boy let loose from school.

"Have you any particular route laid out, Cameron?" asked the old man, as he climbed contentedly into the big car. Because if you haven't I'd like it very much if you would take in Morningside. I saw an old friend this morning who lives out there, and I promised I'd stop in for a greeting if possible."

Cameron Stewart suppressed a twinkle from his eyes and smiled genially.

"All right," he said heartily, "it won't be much out of the way. But we'll take the Park Drive first and come home by Morningside way. I want you to get the full effect of the afternoon light on the woods along the Park

Drive. We'll get over to Morningside a little after four o'clock. Will that be time enough?"

"Oh, plenty!" said the older man and hastened to change the subject.

"Well, here we are," said Stewart, at last, two hours later. "This is Morningside. Did you say Harvard avenue? The last house? Now, shall I run around the block while you go in, or will you be right out again?"

"You come in, Cameron, I very much wish it," said the professor in the tone he used in class when the students tried to beg off. "You know I like my friends to know one another."

The old man's hand was on his arm. Stewart turned away to hide a smile.

"All right if you say so," he answered.

He followed up the path to the familiar door.

The old man did not wait to ring the bell: He walked right in and straight through the hall into the dining-room, looking happily around the while as if he were about to open up some secret delight.

"Ah! Here you are!" came his voice from the room beyond the dining-room. "This way, Cameron. Step right through here!"

Elsie took off her big apron, and turned down the skirt of her green linen gown that had been pinned up under her apron.

The slanting rays of the afternoon sun fell through the wide kitchen window and shone full upon her hair like a halo of blessing as she stooped to take the last loaf of golden crusted bread from the oven. The odor of the fresh bread was floating all about her. On the clean new shelf that ran across one side of the kitchen stood the other loaves across their pans to cool, beside the sponge cake and the pies. A great pan of beans, brown and inviting, stood near, and a generous glass bowl of mayonnaise added its golden hue to the pretty array. It was a sight of which any cook might have been proud.

"We did not stop till we found you, my dear," said Professor Bowen, "and Elsie, child, this is my dear boy, Cameron Stewart. You remember him, I am sure. I have been anxious to have you know one another better."

Stewart came forward smiling.

Professor Bowen stood an instant glancing about the neat kitchen while Elsie and Cameron smiled a greeting over his head. Then turning to the young man suddenly the old professor began to recite: "'After all, these school tests are not real. It's the after life that is the real test, the home life.' Cameron, do you remember saying you would like to see this young woman tried by the fire in the range? Look there!" and he pointed a triumphant finger to the table of inviting cookery.

"I wish it were my pleasant duty to award you your degree," said Stewart gracefully with a smile in his eyes.

"He means he would like to sample your cookery, Elsie," said Professor Bowen comically.

"And so he shall," said Elsie magnanimously. "Where will you begin?"

Cameron Stewart stepped forward and surveyed the row of good things gravely.

"That bread smells delightful," said he, soberly, "but on the whole I think I'll simply have to have a piece of that blackberry pie. I haven't seen blackberry pie like that since I left home."

"You shall have it," said Elsie, proud that she might show what she could do in the line of cookery to both the men. "Just step into the living-room and sit down. Refreshments will be served in three minutes."

Professor Bowen led the way back and they sat down gravely and waited, the elder man gazing about on the pretty room and talking soberly about architecture, with eyes that were twinkling and running over with merriment and "I-told-you-sos." He gave Cameron Stewart no opportunity to interrupt him until in an incredibly short space of time, Elsie appeared with a tray on which was a dainty little repast for two. A crust of the fresh hot bread, a square of butter, a lettuce leaf with a dab of mayonnaise, a dish of the baked beans perfectly browned, a piece of glowing succulent berry pie, with a cup of coffee and a square of golden sponge cake.

"This is the best meal I ever tasted," declared Cameron Stewart as he finished his generous piece of pie and picked up the last crumb of cake. "You get perfect marks from me in every one, if I am allowed to be the judge. And now, most beloved of professors, lest you attempt to rub it in, let me tell you that I have already made my apology for past offences and been forgiven. Professor Bowen, your honor girl is my honor girl, too!"

A little later as they started away, Elsie came out to the car to see them off. As the voice of the engine began to throb, Professor Bowen leaned over the side of the car and whispered to Elsie:

"Good-night, little honor girl—*my* honor girl. I knew you would win!"

About the Author

Grace Livingston Hill is well known as one of the most prolific writers of romantic fiction. Her personal life was fraught with joys and sorrows not unlike those experienced by many of her fictional heroines.

Born in Wellsville, New York, Grace nearly died during the first hours of life. But her loving parents and friends turned to God in prayer. She survived miraculously, thus her thankful father named her Grace.

Grace was always close to her father, a Presbyterian minister, and her mother, a published writer. It was from them that she learned the art of storytelling. When Grace was twelve, a close aunt surprised her with a hardbound, illustrated copy of one of Grace's stories. This was the beginning of Grace's journey into being a published author.

In 1892 Grace married Fred Hill, a young minister, and they soon had two lovely young daughters. Then came 1901, a difficult year for Grace—the year when, within months of each other, both her father and husband died. Suddenly Grace had to find a new place to live (her home was owned by the church where her husband had been pastor). It was a struggle for Grace to raise her young daughters alone, but through everything she kept writing. In 1902 she produced *The Angel of His Presence, The Story of a Whim,* and *An Unwilling Guest*. In 1903 her two books *According to the Pattern* and *Because of Stephen* were published.

It wasn't long before Grace was a well-known author, but she wanted to go beyond just entertaining her readers. She soon included the message of God's salvation through Jesus Christ in each of her books. For Grace, the most important thing she did was not write books but share the message of salvation, a message she felt God wanted her to share through the abilities he had given her.

In all, Grace Livingston Hill wrote more than one hundred books, all of which have sold thousands of copies and have touched the lives of readers around the world with their message of "enduring love" and the true way to lasting happiness: a relationship with God through his Son, Jesus Christ.

In an interview shortly before her death, Grace's devotion to her Lord still shone clear. She commented that whatever she had accomplished had been God's doing. She was only his servant, one who had tried to follow his teaching in all her thoughts and writing.

Don't miss these Grace Livingston Hill romance novels!

VOL.	TITLE	ORDER NUM.
1	Where Two Ways Met	07-8203-8-HILC
2	Bright Arrows	07-0380-4-HILC
3	A Girl to Come Home To	07-1017-7-HILC
4	Amorelle	07-0310-3-HILC
5	Kerry	07-2044-X-HILC
6	All through the Night	07-0018-X-HILC
7	The Best Man	07-0371-5-HILC
8	Ariel Custer	07-1686-8-HILC
9	The Girl of the Woods	07-1016-9-HILC
10	Crimson Roses	07-0481-9-HILC
11	More Than Conqueror	07-4559-0-HILC
12	Head of the House	07-1309-5-HILC
13	In Tune with Wedding Bells	07-1641-8-HILC
14	Stranger within the Gates	07-6441-2-HILC
15	Marigold	07-4037-8-HILC
16	Rainbow Cottage	07-5731-9-HILC
19	Daphne Deane	07-0529-7-HILC
20	The Substitute Guest	07-6447-1-HILC
21	The War Romance of the Salvation Army	07-7911-8-HILC
22	Rose Galbraith	07-5726-2-HILC
24	By Way of the Silverthorns	07-0341-3-HILC
25	Sunrise	07-5941-9-HILC
26	The Seventh Hour	07-5884-6-HILC
27	April Gold	07-0011-2-HILC
28	White Orchids	07-8150-3-HILC
29	Homing	07-1494-6-HILC
30	Matched Pearls	07-3895-0-HILC
32	Coming through the Rye	07-0357-X-HILC
33	Happiness Hill	07-1487-3-HILC
34	The Patch of Blue	07-4809-3-HILC
36	Patricia	07-4814-X-HILC
37	Silver Wings	07-5914-1-HILC
38	Spice Box	07-5939-7-HILC
39	The Search	07-5831-5-HILC

VOL.	TITLE	ORDER NUM.
40	The Tryst	07-7340-3-HILC
41	Blue Ruin	07-0349-9-HILC
42	A New Name	07-4718-6-HILC
43	Dawn of the Morning	07-0530-0-HILC
44	The Beloved Stranger	07-0303-0-HILC
45	The Gold Shoe	07-1101-7-HILC
46	Through These Fires	07-7095-1-HILC
47	The Street of the City	07-5940-0-HILC
48	Beauty for Ashes	07-1220-X-HILC
49	The Enchanted Barn	07-1124-6-HILC
50	The Finding of Jasper Holt	07-0886-5-HILC
51	The Red Signal	07-5402-6-HILC
52	Tomorrow About This Time	07-7186-9-HILC
53	Job's Niece	07-1145-9-HILC
54	The Obsession of Victoria Gracen	07-5050-0-HILC
55	Ladybird	07-2081-4-HILC
56	The Prodigal Girl	07-5039-X-HILC
57	The Honor Girl	07-1390-7-HILC
58	The Chance of a Lifetime	07-1112-2-HILC
59	Astra	07-1214-5-HILC
60	Miranda	07-4298-2-HILC
61	Mystery Flowers	07-4613-9-HILC
63	The Man of the Desert	07-3955-8-HILC
64	Miss Lavinia's Call	07-4360-1-HILC
65	An Unwilling Guest	07-7772-7-HILC
66	The Girl from Montana	07-1051-7-HILC
67	A Daily Rate	07-1247-1-HILC
68	The Story of a Whim	07-6584-2-HILC
69	According to the Pattern	07-1237-4-HILC
70	In the Way	07-1635-3-HILC
71	Exit Betty	07-1285-4-HILC
72	The White Lady	07-8029-9-HILC
73	Not Under the Law	07-4584-1-HILC
74	Lo, Michael	07-2066-0-HILC
75	The Witness	07-8025-6-HILC
76	The City of Fire	07-1244-7-HILC
77	The Ransom	07-5143-4-HILC
79	The Big Blue Soldier	07-0374-X-HILC
80	The Challengers	07-0362-6-HILC

VOL.	TITLE	ORDER NUM.
81	Duskin	07-0574-2-HILC
83	Marcia Schuyler	07-4036-X-HILC
84	Cloudy Jewel	07-0474-6-HILC
85	Crimson Mountain	07-0472-X-HILC
86	The Mystery of Mary	07-4632-5-HILC
87	Out of the Storm	07-4778-X-HILC
88	Phoebe Deane	07-5033-0-HILC
89	Re-Creations	07-5334-8-HILC
90	Sound of the Trumpet	07-6107-3-HILC
91	A Voice in the Wilderness	07-7908-8-HILC
92	The Honeymoon House	07-1393-1-HILC
93	Katharine's Yesterday	07-2038-5-HILC